Dancing on the Beach

Sam Grant

Published by Sam Grant

Publishing partner: Paragon Publishing, Rothersthorpe

Second edition
© Sam Grant 2023

ISBN 978-1-78222-431-0

Book design, layout and production management by Into Print
www.intoprint.net
+44 (0)1604 832149

Chapter 1

WAVES GAVE PROTRACTED SIGH like gasps as they dragged back sand and shingle. You might say to yourself the tide was not rising, but then one determined wave, would hiss and bubble over a previously dry stretch of beach. I was sitting on a row of steps behind a raised mound of white pebble to resist spring tides. For nearly a fortnight I had made the daily sojourn to the beach. It was a chance opportunity. Alfie apparently died suddenly one afternoon, after a heart attack. I was drawing portraits of visitors for a fiver on the cliff path earlier, before applying for the post. He was found by holiday makers, lying face down on the pebbles, behind a boulder. This created a deck chair attendant vacancy in the middle of June. The beach inspector, Bill Simpson, dismissive about Alfie's death, when I applied and got the vacancy.

'Should've taken it easy, with a disability pension from the fire service.' Alfie, was retired early from the service due to smoke inhalation aged forty-five. He started as a deck chair attendant the previous season. The other guys, said to me later that he liked the job come rain or shine. No close family in the vicinity after his foster parents went to Australia. He trained to be a fireman in his twenties, but I found out later that he started his working life as a fisherman, aboard a local trawler out of Paignton.

During my first week, Bill Simpson said he went with the police to Alfie's flat. The council received the uniform back from the mortuary, together with personal possessions, including a wrist watch, a half roll of Polo mints, pocket book with name and address, a wallet containing some loose change and his phone containing pictures of his cat. There was a key fob with a Yale key: the key to the flat. Bill conveyed this information to me while in the office, cashing up tickets sold for the day.

'He lived in a flat down York Avenue, above the beach,' said Bill. I was writing the five-figure number from the ticket machine above the start number for the day to arrive at a sales number, while Bill told me about Alfie's back story. Inspectors and managers can be willing to share confidences with new employees, who are not that enmeshed into workplace realities, acquired when working with a more cynical and dissbelieving workforce.

'The two of us that's me and the sergeant went to the bedsit.' He wanted to tell me all about what happened. 'The neighbor, in the flat next door must've heard the door open to Alfie's flat.'

'I knew something was up,' she said to me, ever so polite, with the sergeant being there.

'That damned cat kept meowing all night in the corridor. Turned its nose up at a bit of chicken. Never known any cat do that before. Good job one of your lads came round,' she said. But she quietened down a lot when the sergeant produced his smart phone and asked for a name to type in. Phil, you don't mind Phil,' he said, as if there is a choice when nearly everyone except for your mother calls you Phil and not Philip.

'No, that's okay,' I said, getting up to hang the ticket machine on the number five hook.

'You know Phil, it was neat and tidy. The breakfast things in the small kitchen washed and on the draining board. The duvet neatly folded in half to air the bed. The sergeant opened the drawers of the dressing table and the clothes inside were neatly folded. Then he twisted the handle on the wardrobe door. There was a shoe box on the top shelf.

The sergeant pulled on it. It slipped from his hand and fell to the floor. Bundles and bundles of banded notes fell on to the floor. There were eighteen. Each bundle was a month's pay. They went back to when he started last year.' Bill's hand, at this point, made a sand effect against his chin, which led to the opening of the filing cabinet drawer and a rifle for battery shaver and shaving mirror. He placed the mirror on the cabinet, which was about level with his face

The shaver's buzz, competed with gulls that squawked and scratched on the hut's roof. I walked to my locker and opened it to get my belongings out; – A carrier bag with a lunch box and Thermos. I was into economy mode and not buying meals at the café.

This afternoon shave, I discovered later, was a preliminary to Bill's visit to Julie at the rail ticket office. It was an appreciation, arrived at from talking to Ingrid, the Polish restaurant manager. I went in to get a Coke and swap a bag full of coins for notes.

'How are you then with working – for Romeo?' she asked 'What do you mean?' I asked all innocent.

'The age it is not the same, but it is for those of us working on the beach, like a Romeo and Juliet story.' I think Ingrid may have got the Romeo bit right, but a resemblance to the Shakespeare play beyond the name Romeo was hard to picture.

'Your inspector chief Bill with Julie. Such a lovely girl.' To me, at the time, more woman than girl.

'An English lady rose. I not see what she like with your inspector They both with partners too. I feel sorry for these. No sex energy for them with romance here in beach kiosk.' I wasn't aware they were at it like rabbits in the ticket booth, but Ingrid seemed to think so.

'What you say Annie?' Annie was about eighteen, and assisted in the restaurant. She stopped momentarily, I remember at the time, and gave a blushing smile, before she tipped a bucket of chips into the fryer. The immediate sizzle drowned out the possibility of reply.

My thoughts returned to the here and now when Bill switched off the battery shaver and returned both shaver and mirror to the filing cabinet. He wasn't for letting me go, though.

'What do you make of that Phil? Took his wages from the bank and stashed the money away. What's he lived on, all that time?'

'Perhaps he had a work pension,' I said. 'Didn't work for money. Perhaps Alfie was putting aside money for his funeral.' I immediately regretted this remark, but Bill said nothing. Alfie's wage saving was outside Bill's orbit of appreciation. He scavenged the beach whenever the tide receded. Chairs were hastily moved back by holidaymakers to keep away from the tides advance – Coins and valuables like, watches, and gold rings were lost in the scramble to get clear of the waves. These could later re-appear near the shore from tidal action. There for Bill to pick out with his eagle eye. He once showed me a barnacle encrusted diamond ring, pound coins and fifty pence pieces darkened by the sea. The swirl of the waves rolled back lost treasure and valuables from seasons past. Any idea that the contents of a wage packet would not be needed, wholly foreign to Bill – that anyone should spend the summer on the beach putting out deck chairs, chatting to holidaymakers and then re-stacking chairs back in a pile at the end of the day, without being in desperate need of money. It was a concept removed from Bill's needy or perhaps seedy world of finance, associated with having a sometime beach mistress—the lovely Julie to look after.

Chapter 2

'BILL, DO YOU WANT coffee or not?' 'What's the matter Julie?'

'Nothings the matter, you haven' t answered my question.' 'Yes, I will, if there's some of those Bourbon biscuits to go with it.

'You' re fussy – think yourself lucky I' m offering, she said with a superior look.

'I was more interested in you,' said Bill. He kissed her on the cheek. Julie moved away to pull down the blind, and bolt the hatch with "Closed" then showing on the outside. She smiled. Traced her fingers down his left arm, and softly said, 'yes,' invitingly. Bill retraced his steps and turned the door key. The split side of the maxi skirt opened, on his return, while she knelt to switch on the kettle.

'Calm down they've left the beach, Terry and his friend,' she said.

The kettle hummed. Julie opened the cupboard door, pulled out a tray, two mugs, an opened packet of bourbons and a carton of milk, which stood in a bucket of iced water from the restaurant. Bill held her waist as she spooned coffee and sugar into the mugs. She held up her index finger and said, 'Wait.' She placed the spoon on the table. With crossed arms and playful look, she removed her jumper. Her bikini top already in the desk drawer. The short break necessitated expedient preparation. Skirt buttons already unbuttoned, meant a one run release of the zip let the skirt fall to the floor, which she picked up before laying it across the filing cabinet, together with the jumper. Light shining from the bulb overhead flicked across Julie's sapphire blue toe nails, in the otherwise darkened office. She held out the packet of Bourbons. 'You' ll be having coffee then?' It was just the coffee and biscuits you came for, was it not?' Bill, stood back a pace or two.

The kettle spurted steam and clicked off. Julie turned sideways to grab the handle. Bill caressed her shoulders and neck above the white line of the removed bikini top.

'Careful, you'll have boiling water over us.' There was never a possibility that the bourbons were the real aphrodisiac, but this pretence was part of the tease satisfaction – for Julie.

'It's okay. Terry left the beach an hour ago,' she said reassuringly. A silver framed photo of the Swedish swimming instructor had already been placed in the office drawer. Memories of Karl's assured, polite manner, still surfaced. He would place a cushion on the lows-slung dining room table, when Terry was away at. She remembered the excitement. Karl always kissed her passionately before his hands gripped her waist. He would then effortlessly lift her on to the cushion at the table edge. There followed an unorthodox polishing of the table with the cushion. Slowly back and forth before speeding up. The cushion like a polisher at work on the table. Bill, nor her husband Terry made the earth move in quite the way Karl did, she considered. The chair in the corner of the kiosk did not match up to this experience of ten years ago. She closed her eyes, momentarily and imagined the taught firm body of Karl, his blond frizzy hair and face every bit as serious as when in a swimming race, and intent on winning. The frisson of having Karl that summer of 2005 as her admirer and boyfriend was never going to be recreated with Bill, but he was attentive and she knew infatuated, which gave her the upper hand. Terry was all dewy eyed over a new young graduate which the company assigned to shadow him hoping more from the trainee than just the shadowing. Julie removed Bill's hands from around her toned bottom, but she turned to smile, not wishing to suggest it was discouraged altogether. More that she needed to safely pour scalding water into the coffee mugs. Bill now stripped to swimming trunks, shirt, and tie. The same light blue colour Karl wore.

'Light blue really turns me on, you know,' she said when

Bill, suggested an afternoon assignation. It was true, but she did not expand on the reason.

'Light blue's the colour which excites me most on a man,' she said again on this occasion. She walked to the side of the desk and removed red bikini briefs, dotted with yellow splotches. Memories of Karl assisted in arousing an appropriate level of excitement. Not so easily obtained when faced with Bill's paunch and bald patch. The hair loss was more apparent without his cap, but not so much when he walked on the beach in his inspector's role. She set her phone alarm for twelve minutes and switched on the radio. Perhaps rail passengers were outside reading the A4 glossy print – out on the closed hatch, which said.

"Your ticket attendant will be with you shortly after the bell rings. We thank you for your patience and understanding during this designated afternoon staff break." Bill planted kisses on her left shoulder, while she stirred the mugs of coffee. He unclipped his tie smiled at Julie, and with unbuttoned shirt eyed the corner chair, but Julie nodded toward two cushions on the floor, strategically placed for best effect. Their last kiosk rendezvous now two days past. A more intense coupling than usual ensued, before Julie's phone alarm jingled. Three minutes earlier than the public bell outside the kiosk. The bright sun prevented anyone peering into the kiosk even with the customer hatch open. Bill retreated to the back with his clothes, coffee and two Bourbons while Julie sat in the kiosk chair.

She retrieved the bikini top from the drawer. The Velcro straps speeded up dress procedure. She grabbed the skirt and zipped it up, then kneeled to inspect face and make up in front of the kiosk mirror, prior to re-applying lipstick. The mirror, inset into the chest of a male swimmer, with fair hair, blue trunks, raised arms and muscular legs leaning – forward as if about to dive on to the floor. She managed a sip of coffee, but returned to the mirror again to ensure that lipstick was un-smudged. With a bell clang, the roller cover flew upwards and open. Rail tickets were once more on sale to the public. There was a back door exit with steps conveniently obscured by the yellow gorse that led Bill directly back on to Babbacombe Beach.

Chapter 3

THE TICKET KIOSK, WHICH overlooked the beach was sited next to the large cream painted station. The double track rail lines were at a steep angle running from the Downs to Babbacombe Beach. The tram like cars, synchronized their arrival at the top and bottom station. Stilt-like metal struts at the front levelled out the carriage for passengers. When first spotted the cars gave the appearance of giraffe like animals, striding up and down from the beach.

Each carriage was secured by cables at the top station. Passengers, waved one to another as cars crossed journeyed up or down from the beach. A red nonslip pavement led down to a small service car park from the cable car station. A boat park, fenced off like a tennis court, against the cliff face contained about forty sailing dinghies. This was next to the prominent centrally positioned blue and white yacht club house A balcony set quite high up, ran across its front. This clubhouse could have passed for a country house on the beach were it not for the display board set between two upstairs windows which stated on a dark blue background. "Babbacombe Corinthian Yacht Club." Flag poles, dotted along the balcony were, also a giveaway. A balcony, which gave a clear view of Babbacombe Bay became a starting gun position for racing, at weekends and summer regattas.

This area was tarmacked, but more friendly red and, grey paved slabs were laid out in front of tented changing cubicles and a row of twenty brightly painted beach huts. Further along, the beach Inspector's office. Timbered like the beach huts, but about ten times larger. It was conveniently placed next to Ingrid's restaurant. In front of the restaurant were tables and chairs with sun brollies. A promenade fronted the restaurant with newish galvanized fencing along its length. Occasional openings with hand rails down the steps allowed access to the beach. The mainly pebbled beach looked white when viewed from the Downs, but nearer, dried seaweed with long storks stretched across patches of the beach, deposited by previous tides. Bill I later discovered was paid a pound a basket for sea weed by a fertilizer company. The transaction took place at the back door of the Inspector's hut. On the easterly side by the promenade the red cliffs looked more solid than those above the pathway, where I previously sketched holidaymakers. I realized at this point that I needed this deck chair work to survive. Before I' d kidded myself that selling sketches to holiday makers would pay the rent on the flat.

My resignation from the bank a month previously meant a big drop in income. I was standing with my arms on the railings by the promenade, when I heard voices behind.

'Come on Phil, they' ll zip down, with not a cloud in the sky, like locusts seeing green on a tree,' Dan shouted. He was walking up from behind with Ian and Barry in tow. I didn't hear their approach. I faced the shore. Waves bubbled on the white pebbles, in front and spilt lazily across the beach before retracting. That latent power like a resting tiger flexing claws out and in. I stood up, turned, and walked towards the other three.

'Phil you can lend a hand with setting up a few chairs before the ferry arrives,' Dan continued.

'And by the way mate there's a beach party coming up a week Saturday, if you've got some Sheila you'd like to bring along.' Dan liked to portray publicly the idea that he might have Australian origin.

'Right Dan,' I said. 'Sounds like fun.' At that point there was no "Sheila" in my life, but that was set to change.

Dan knelt before the hut like structure of chairs, unlocked the padlock, which held the light chain wrapped twice around the tarpaulin. When Ian and Barry tugged at the tarpaulin from the other side it released a puddle of water on to Dan, who neatly stepped to one side to miss a soaking of his beach uniform and rolled up trousers. The ferry was due in at nine. Dan was the self-appointed leader of the group. Ian and Barry were old hands from the beginning of the season. I was still a novice in my second week.

'Okay, give you ten minutes, then,' I said when I arrived at the deck chair stack. Ian scrambled up the short ladder taken out from beneath the tarpaulin. There was a pattern you might say to the un-stacking. The one on top threw a chair down to be caught by the two beneath. The fourth one, in this case me, picked up a chair to set up along the front. The technique was to shake open the chair in a way that forced the hinged bar to slot into the ridged grooves on the outer struts. I could flip an opened chair back. Catch, and take hold of the folded frame, but lacked the dexterity and speed in the process of putting a chair up to make it look effortless. The others could fling open the chair with one hand and make it stand with just a foot kick. After five minutes of catching chairs Dan and Barry prepared stacks of four to carry into position. Soon there were six of these stacks spaced along the front to my only fourth opened chair.

'How many Dan, called out Barry.' 'Let's go for three rows of twenty.

By the time the others finished piling the stacks I was near to putting up ten chairs. Barry from the Midlands was unable to resist saying,

'Good job you're not on piece work Phil, there would not be much in your pay packet. It was not meant to offend. Before long I mastered the skills of the other three and then it was never an issue. The tide was high up on to the first run of pebbles, but as it fell back the sun would pop over the cliffs above. The visitors were then likely to take chairs to the beach. The winch drum whirred, and started to lower the landing stage from the concrete slip. The brake rasped intermittently when the winch man lowered the brake lever to put a check on the Landing Stage's journey to the sea. It was a fine judgement not to hold it back over much. Momentum was needed to let it run across the pebbles. It looked like a giant crocodile waddling down the beach. The planked embarkation gangway with wooden steps held up by chains, either side in place of the teeth of a wide-open jaw. There was a booking office, like a large garden shed half way along the planked walkway. Buoyancy tanks fitted underneath allowed it to float once in the water. Beneath the ticket office and thirty-foot walkway, axles joined three pairs of lorry sized wheels. The perimeter of the landing stage fenced with double gates at the front to allow passengers from the ferry to disembark, but also to allow access to pedalos' and rafts, which were tethered to moorings close to the Landing Stage. I stopped putting up deck chairs to watch this creaking structure move from the slipway to the beach. I watched as visitors walked the short distance from the railway carriage to the tarmacked beach front. The beach was empty save for Bill. The ferry ticket collector was now the winch man at the top of the beach. Bill, visible to him hand – signaling whether to brake or release the cable, which governed the descent of the Landing Stage. Bill, then shouted back up from halfway down the beach.

'Let it go now Jack,' while making a repeated forward wave with his raised right hand. This allowed the landing stage to gather momentum before it plunged in. It splashed noisily into the sea. The main walkway slowed and settled with rubber fenders visible. Bill, walked out in waders to grab a coiled line to secure the landing stage, before unshackling the winch wire. He circled his arm for the winch man to reverse and retrieve both wire and shackle. Holding ropes secured to the stage on each side were fed through steel hooped concrete blocks pegged into the beach. These led up the beach to accommodate tide levels.

The ferry boat's white hull appeared around the cliffs shortly after the stage was in place. A forty-foot open boat with a sizeable twin port holed, decked fo'c'sle, running aft from the bow. The steering wheel and throttle attached to the mid-ships' engine housing. Blue smoke from the exhaust hovered over the red ensign flag at the stern. I counted five passengers, sat well back from the bow. Bill Simpson turned and cupped his hands.

'Have you got the truck ready?' I waved in acknowledgement and went to fetch it from behind a deck chair stack. The sun flashed across the white hull of the ferry, momentarily, before it plunged into the shadow formed from the seventy-metre-high red cliffs, which surrounded the pebbled beach. I noticed the white crisp bow wave disappear as the skipper throttled back for his approach to the Landing Stage. 'See you guys,' I called out as the flat bed electric truck whirred across the tarmac, down the slipway and on to the beach. The pneumatic tyres bounced over the pebbles on the way to the landing stage. The passengers disembarked before I reached the stage. The cool boxes to be unloaded were made of a sturdy white polystyrene with the word "cool box" labelled on the sides. Four clips on top secured the lid. Webbed strap handles, attached either side enabled them to be lifted out like a shopping basket.

I ran the truck up on to the landing stage, while the ferry crewman pulled away the canvas across the cool boxes stacked in the after deck. The trolley allowed two layers of ten to be stacked within the wire cage, which prevented any from falling out. I grabbed the handles of the boxes as they were handed across from the ferry. Within ten minutes they were all in the trolley. I backed it down the ramp. and crawled up the beach, with its motor humming at a higher pitch than when empty. I left the beach, via the slipway and followed the path leading to the railway.

Chapter 4

THE GREEN PAINTED ROOF of the cable car station contrasted with its cream walls. The cars were stopped by buffers inside the building, which made a wheezing sound like that from lorry brakes, but slower and less emphatic. A car arrived just as I reached the ticket kiosk A few seconds elapsed between its arrival and its final resting place. I stopped the electric trolley opposite the ticket office.

'Going up for a free breakfast at Sea View, then?' asked Julie, who was leant forward from inside the kiosk hatch. The white framed sunglasses on her forehead, matched the tee shirt, which let through evidence of a skimpy red bikini top underneath. Julie was both friendly and attractive. Especially so to a man in his forties, like Bill, I considered.

'You must be joking – I wish I was, though,' I said in reply. 'Miss the sketching?' She asked, with a smile. Word must have got around.

'Sometimes,' I said. The cab doors opened with that gasp like sound. Moments later holidaymakers swirled around the trolley on their way to the beach. I caught a hand wave from Julie, while she answered a couple's questions, who stopped outside the kiosk. The carriage's compression against the buffers caused valves to open and allowed water to drain away. Tanks in the bottom of the carriage were water filled at the top station to ensure a gravitational weight advantage. This enabled the carriage, me, and the electric trolley and passengers' to be pulled back up the slope. There were rows of straps for standing passengers to hold on to, but the four centre seats could be released to slide into the sides of the carriage and fastened. This allowed floor space for the electric truck. Passenger space then limited to about six adults, including myself and the conductor, who stood at the front. The doors opened on the opposite end at the top. There could be a look of disappointment on the faces of beach goers waiting to board the cliff rail carriage, when the trolley filled the centre space.

'Thought this was for passengers, not freight. We' d have stayed another half hour on the beach if we' d known that truck was being loaded,' one lobster red holidaymaker said. Most were more understanding. A few days of sunny weather could help their disposition.

The trolleys speed up the road from the top of the railway to the front of the Downs went from about three to two mph, even with the batteries fully charged. I looked back to the closed pathway that led to the beach with the groups of visitors compelled to walk on the road, if they did not take the carriage. A sign mounted above the improvised fencing that blocked the path, stated:

NO ENTRY TO THE PUBLIC
SEVERE ROCK FALL
VISITORS TO THE BEACH ARE ADVISED
TO WALK ON THE RIGHT SIDE OF THE ROAD
GOING TO AND FROM THE BEACH

The rock fall of over a fortnight ago was life changing. Not that I was there when it happened! But it ended my self-employment of pencil sketching visitors on the path as they went to and from the beach. I spotted an "A" board outside the cliff railway, advertising for a deck chair attendant and applied. The 8 am start – a shock to the system for an itinerant artist, who picked those days to sketch only when there was a serious cash flow problem, during summer months. Barry, however, ever ready to comment on my good fortune, as he saw it, said,

'You' re dead lucky to get that job. I put my name down in February and only just got taken on. They queue up from where I come from to get a job like this. Summer by the seaside chatting to holidaymakers and getting a tan. Paid as well.'

I did not mention how I was quite happy penciling about four sketches a day for a fiver each. Even if it meant sketching a yapping dog or an attractive woman who was usually pleased—but, not necessarily the boyfriend or partner. One of whom made me tear the portrait up, without giving a reason. The girl, said nothing, but on the way back from the beach, smiled and sneaked me a five-pound note. I liked to think it was more to do with their relationship or lack of, than my sketching of her in a bikini top and jeans. That was all in the past, though.

There were usually two weekly visits to the hotel with dairy supplies. Fierce sculptured birds on the top of pillars splattered with yellow lichen led into Sea View. The wings outstretched. Mythological conception rather than copies from nature. These two exaggerated eagle-like birds with fearsome curved beaks. Over large talons straddled the concrete globes, which they were on. The marauding herring gulls were unaffected by their presence, since they treated outside the hotel roof, and garden as their own estate. They were ever ready to vacate the front garden for polystyrene food containers. They snatched the contents from boxes held by unwary visitors, who walked by on the front. The gull's interpretation of take away, not the one intended. This was my second weekly visit to Sea View Hotel. I waved my hand in thanks as the electric truck crawled along the road and oncoming traffic was required to stop to allow me across to the hotel entrance. A few gulls flew into the air, with a defiant squawk as I entered the garden on my way to the kitchens at the back. They more annoyed at my presence than in any way fearful. I released the broad webbed straps that secured the boxes and knocked on the kitchen door. Empty containers were stacked at the side. A red wheeled hand truck stood against the wall outside the hotel cold storage room.

The Spanish chef's large red face appeared from behind the kitchen door.

'It is zee cool boxes, they arrive Joe.' Joe, an ex-serviceman with one good arm and the other with a hook appeared in the doorway.

'Ah the milkman disguised as a deck chair attendant. Not too rough out there, I hope. One day that cream's going to be butter,' he said. There was always some whimsical comment from Joe. I loaded four boxes at a time on to the hand truck for him to wheel into the cold room

'They' re twenty, you make sure, Joe,' I heard the chef say as Joe went into the kitchen to get a signature.

I still required the hotel stamp on the delivery note and left Joe to load the return cool boxes on to the trolley, while I walked through the kitchens. I caught the appetizing smell of freshly baked rolls when a tray was removed from an oven to cool. The seared smell of grilled kippers intermingled with bacon crisping under an adjacent grill. Breakfast for the guests was still in full swing – the tease to my stomach unfair. My earlier breakfast in the flat now seemed to inhabit a long distant epoch in history. The flat was in a Victorian three-story building. The landlord squeezed five flats into it. It was a far cry from the ground floor flat in the three bedroomed semi that I shared with a newly married couple in Grove Green on the outskirts of London. There, we shared the kitchen, but there was a separate downstairs bath room. It was affordable then on a bank salary even though rents were high with proximity to the capital.

Enjoyable family holidays during child hood decided me on a summer in Babbacombe, after resigning from the bank. Home was in Harpenden, Herts, but it was a case of have car can travel after working a month's notice. I knew it would not be welcome news that I had given in my notice at the bank at my parent's house. I still maintained thoughts about a return to art college.

'They'll always need banks,' and people to work in them was my father's view. I knew Babbacombe and the Downs quite well. The Victorian house along Acacia Avenue advertised flats online. I remembered walking past the house on the way to a self -catering flat in Cary Park, which was owned by aunt Sybil. My mother grew up in Babbacombe and liked to catch up on family news from her sister, who was now sadly deceased. The move to Babbacombe was not really a step forward, but more a breathing space for the Summer.

Chapter 5

A SHORT CORRIDOR FROM the kitchen led to the breakfast room – a timbered glass extension set out with tables – shielded from both the kitchen and reception area by miniature palms placed against a tall glass screen with sail boat pictures. I moved to one side as a waitress, holding a tray with racks of triangular toast in silver stands went by. Even the aroma of toast smelt like nectar for the gods, on its own. I heard a mixture of voices, young and old and the clatter of knives, forks, as I approached the reception. Pamela the Asian receptionist, stretched forwards to place keys on hooks, as she answered the phone. She must have sensed my being there and turned, to smile, while silently moving her lips and saying, 'just a minute,' while pointing, at the phone. Her slim figure sheathed in a white sleeveless mini dress splattered with red roses, dark hair flowed partly on to one shoulder. Her attractiveness was more accentuated than when I first saw her sat at the desk, in a navy business suit, with severely coiffured hair. The smile further enhanced her attractiveness, but in a daunting – out of my league sort of way. It was then that I chanced to hear the conversation between John Langridge the hotel owner and a guest, standing opposite in the window alcove. Hands moved together and apart again giving undivided attention to his obviously important guest, while he slowly nodded his head to further emphasis understanding and agreement. My hearing was sharp. There were sideways looks. First by John Langridge, and then his guest. This implied secretiveness. But I could hear every word said. 'Friday, Saturday and away on Sunday. Every weekend for the next two months. I can trust you to keep a secret John, I'm sure.' I could not see the inside of the leather card holder that he opened in front of John, but heard his reply after he looked down at it.

'Yes, Chief Inspector,' he said, in recognition of the now revealed status.

'Well, that's it John, CID would rather I didn't reveal my identity. I'd prefer it if you continued with always identifying me as James Watson, area manager for S&H premier cake distribution – visiting outlets in the vicinity of Babbacombe. You understand I'm undercover as far as the public's concerned.

You can call me Jim, Jim Watson that's perfectly acceptable.

'Of course, Mr Watson. I mean Jim. You can be assured that it will go no further.'

Was I invisible? The answer to that was yes, in the way that countless workers went about their daily tasks and were believed to be part of the furniture uninterested in anything going on. Part of the furniture around other's lives, you might say.

'Phil-ip.' I loved immediately the way she said my name with a raised inflection on the final syllable.

'Have you got the invoice for me to stamp?' Pamela walked across to stand opposite. She produced a self-inking hotel stamp. I faced the invoice towards her on the desk. I'd never told her my name, but doubtless John Langridge had. It was after the stamp made that ratchet like sound and her hand collapsed it on to the invoice and back, that I blurted out.

'Would you like to go out? I mean do you have an evening free?' extending the request not wanting obviously to receive a point-blank refusal.

'I know we've like only just met. Not immediately, I mean.' I was caught in that abyss of vulnerability, where the rejection slip can so easily be handed out by a woman. She was studying the invoice in a way that made me think that the answer was written on it in some code before handing it back.

'What is wrong with immediately. Are you going away somewhere?' It was in part the wonderful way foreign girls, can sometimes confuse the nuances of words, where they might understand the translation, but get the context mixed.

Pamela's spoken English was perfect. It was probably more related to Asian culture and approach to relationships.

'Nothing wrong with immediately, except we're both working.' I replied.

'Yes, I know that, but you're speaking as if there's something else you have to do. You don't already have girlfriend?'

'No. Why? Why would I ask you out?'

'That's okay, then Phil-ip. I finish here, after teas are served.'

'Four o'clock?'

'No five. I'll be ready at seven. Where are you taking me?' This was moving on like a steam train. Pamela must have been about twenty-four. About, the same age as me, but more self-assured than other girls about calling the shots. Usually, you had to accommodate a deliberate kind of delay by a girl, who teased with your emotions. You, like an interviewee left outside of an outright answer. Left apprehensive. Unsure how well you're request for a date's been received, if at all. It did seem that she somehow knew that I would ask her out. Not now meeting that disappointment of rejection, I relaxed a bit. The thing was, you did not necessarily get an outright, "no." There was the "I can't, not at the moment" or "I don't think I can," which was intended to make you believe that she was already in a relationship and unavailable or far too studiously engaged in a course of study to even consider men. Not maybe that they could not stand the sight of you or preferred partnering their own sex. Life was then full of unexpected twists and turns in the matter of boy, girl relationships.

You always thought the one that wasn't interested in you had something special on offer, but it could be a dangerous game to play hard to get once your heart took the decision to go for it—without so much as having a rain check on whether there was a real chance!

'There's the Blue Comet Night Club.' I'd been caught on the hop.

'We could go there after going to a pub,' I said. The Blue Comet was at the far end of the Downs.

'A pub in town?' she asked.

'No, I've a car we could drive out somewhere.' Her eyes lightened at this suggestion.

'See you outside the hotel at seven then, Phil-ip. I have work to do now. The "area manager for S&H Distribution" came over holding a key with a brass fob, which he placed on the desk next to Pamela. He removed a newspaper from the stacked row on the reception desk and started flicking through the pages. I left through the kitchen.

Chapter 6

AFTER PHIL, LEFT THE foyer of the hotel, sound of talk from the breakfast room took over.

With view of the sea from Babbacombe Downs, carpeted blue and the sky, home only to the odd wisp of horses' tail. Hotel guests would not linger indoors.

'No problem you can still get to the empty boxes?' Mr Watson, continued turning the pages while he spoke.

'Yes, papa they will be in the same place as before, in the outer pantry, next to the fridges.'

'Do not call me papa again, in the hotel.'

'Just a slip. It won't happen again. You do not want to be called Chief Inspector either then?' Continued Pamela with a facetious smile, that he pretended not to notice. She knew that he was right, but then he needn't have snapped.

'No Meila. You know it's the disguise I use to impress the hotel manager. I am signed in as James Watson and the other role is to be kept secret.'

'Touche,' then said Pamela.

'You can't be calling me Meila, either!'

'All right, that makes it all square.' He folded the newspaper and returned it to the stack, after Pamela pointed her finger in that direction.

Meila was Pamela's birth name in Hong Kong. Both mother and daughter adopted English names when they first arrived in Britain. Her father, Alex Tomkins, was like a chameleon about names. Her mother's Hong Kong name was Ling, but she altered it to Rita, which she preferred. Meila, changed her name to Pamela, but she preferred Meila and would give this as her name to friends. They stopped talking when a woman handed a room key to Pamela.

'Have a nice day,' Pamela, said and smiled. She waited for her to be out of earshot before she returned to talking with her father.

'I've got to fetch the milk for the afternoon-teas. It is quiet and packets can easily be removed without anyone noticing. There is, a new person, who delivers cool boxes from the beach, after the old man died.'

'It's accepted that the deck chair attendant died of a heart attack. That he died a natural death,' said her father, who looked up from the paper.

'It would be weird if it wasn't,' said Pamela.

The smuggling of Cocaine from the cruise ships into Sea View reconciled for Pamela by the fact that customers pay good money for drugs, and they were going to buy them, regardless of who sold them. Her father's stay at Sea View was a double bluff. She knew, that he was planning to fool the manager into believing he was police CID and spotted this in progress earlier. Aware that Phillip also heard and saw this as well, in the alcove in front of reception.

Pamela was previously in banking and made out that she disliked the macho culture of investment banking, but she learnt to understand how money talks, whether through legitimate investment or drug sales. It was about getting a flow of profit her father accrued, into legitimate capital assets. She could advise him financially and maintained contacts through the investment arm of her former employer Loyalty Bank. There were few investments that could give such consistently high returns, year in year out like the selling on of Cocaine. Her mother never understood the level of complicity between father and daughter. Like her father Pamela liked to shape shift into roles. Prepared to sacrifice immediate acquisition of wealth and to take a job as receptionist, for example. Her father was, to all intents and purposes, a successful share trader, who made a killing before moving out of London. Rita, a former dress designer sold her boutique and was now looking for new premises by the seaside. The move was in March, just after Pamela left the investment bank. It was mother Rita, who found the receptionists position at Sea View for Pamela, but was fed the idea by Alex.

The Sea View Hotel was decided to be a reception point for consignments of drugs smuggled ashore via the Babbacombe beach ferry service. But it was Pamela, who suggested that drug profits would be invested to buy gold sovereigns. Then to be deposited in random banks in five thousand -pound tranches. Her mother initially knew nothing about the drugs side of the business, but was made aware of it just before they made the move out of London to live in Babbacombe.

She held her own bank account, and to an extent was self-financing, but was brought around to an acceptance that Alex traded as he put it – in illicit substances – by the promise of a new dress boutique, where Alex would pay for the lease and stock it. Palms, along the way were greased to ensure awkward questions were never asked. Alex Tompkins was, in a sense, a distribution manager, but for bundles of Cocaine. Not, for S&H and their high-class cakes and confectionery. Beach inspector, Bill Simson at Babbacombe, was one such greased palm. He did not know that drugs were stashed in the bottom of the cool boxes, but the thousand pounds, which entered his bank account every month, meant that he never asked awkward questions. He believed that any smuggling involved tobacco and spirit duty evasion. There can be an ambivalence about this form of smuggling.

Pamela was not an innocent participant. Beauty in a woman is often admired, and her charms sought. The allure not necessarily a premise for the absence of evil. Pamela or Meila as she preferred to be called by close friends did not then appreciate the extent of her father's ruthlessness, when first she accepted the position of receptionist at the Sea View Hotel. Manager John Langridge, seemed to have no direct connection with her father, that she knew about.

He pushed open the double doors, which led from break-fast room to foyer, while he held a tray of silver tea and coffee pots. Turned to face her father and said,

'Is everything all right Mr Watson, I mean Jim?'

Alex, furrowed his brow and looked confidentially at the manager.

'John, I would like to leave a case in a secure place here in the hotel. I have important documents, which need to be safe, while out on business, in the area, you understand, he said.

'It will be my pleasure, I perfectly understand. There are secrets in business that need to be kept locked away. Pamela, Mr Watson is area manager for S and H the premier cake manufacturer. He turned back to Alex. Pamela will see that the case goes straight into our safe.'

'Excellent, excellent.' Pamela smiled dutifully. The hotel manager's self-importance enhanced by being a sharer of secret information. That, to him, Mr Watson was a Chief Inspector with CID. Pamela's employment was that of receptionist plus that of the provision of morning coffees for residents and non-residents. A day, which ended with the laying out of tables for afternoon teas.

'I'll be able to leave the case overnight and collect it in the morning for the time I'm here, then John?' asked Mr Watson.

'But of course, but of course.'

For Pamela this was an altogether better arrangement. Previously she took the sachets to her father's room and put them in the case. Now they could be placed straight into it. Mr Langridge had entrusted her with the full six numbered combination code to open the safe.

'You do not need to call me over. I would rather Mr Watson can have immediate access, but if you need to access customers belongings call me Pamela. It is better that they see two members of staff are required to open the safe,' he said. Pamela went along with this. She could see her father was given high priority, but this was now perhaps because he was not only a regular stay guest, but also a Chief Inspector of police.

Come late afternoon and there was no one about. Mr Langridge would partake in a siesta and the guests not yet returned from beach. While cruise ships were in and out of Babbacome Bay a continuous stream of sachets could be delivered to the hotel in the bases of the dairy cool boxes. Her father filtered some proceeds into the Blue Comet night club, where he held a seventy-five per cent stake. That is what he told her. The family moved in 2005 from Hong Kong to a spacious country house in Surrey. After school Pamela helped in her mother's dress boutiques. Then she went to university. After university, she worked for three years at an investment bank, but left in February.

On returning to her parent's home, she discovered that her mother no longer had the boutique. Father no longer traded shares. Everything was sold. Her mother said,

'It is in the floor of the Range Rover. A man strengthened the floor. They are under the seats and in the back.'

'What are?' asked Pamela, not understanding what her mother meant.

'Gold bars, like chocolate bars. Your father had all the gold melted down into thousand-pound value ingots. He said, that he was finished with City paper and electronic money and that would we like to move to the seaside. You've always liked the beaches and swimming Pamela and it will be helpful for us to be seen as just ordinary.'

'What do you mean, we are ordinary?'

'No, I mean ordinary and not too clever. I am going to start a new business at the seaside, but first we become ordinary. Pamela, papa knows you like boutiques.'

'Don't include me in your dream world of boutiques. 'Your father's, starting a new venture. We will be able to expand into dress shops, and perhaps other business – like buy to let for the rich old people, who live by the seaside. You might even find a husband. Who knows? Pamela's father was a lot less than scrupulously honest, and a month before graduation he sent

29

a cheque for forty thousand pounds to clear a student debt.

'Rather you than the tax man,' he wrote in a short note wrapped around the cheque. She started at an investment bank after graduation, three years ago. But would tell anyone who asked that she did not care for the macho culture. Her mother was keen to get her settled for the summer, at least.

'He would like it very much, if you agreed to take a little job for the summer at a hotel, as a receptionist. It will be with special duties, but you are clever and he will be there. His business requires him to stay there incognito. Is that the word? That no one really knows who he is.

'Probably,' said Pamela. You mean he will have a role and a name, but it will not be Alex Tomkins.'

'Yes, that's it. He'll not be known as your father.' 'Sounds okay to me,' said Pamela, who knew her father adopted a persona for his clandestine activities.

'It is this one. This hotel. Her mother brought an advert for a receptionist up on her I-pad, beneath a picture of Sea View Hotel, Babbacombe.

'It's all right you can apply Pamela. I've made enquiries. The manager's said that he is keen for you to apply, which is as good as saying you have the job. That's how it came about. Pamela went along with her mother's suggestion, but then her father previously messaged her about working with him at Sea View.

Chapter 7

MID-AFTERNOON ON THE BEACH and the sun beat down. Tarmac trickled in the heat—entered its stench into the cockpit of beach smells. Seaweed, vanilla ices, cigarette smoke plus perfume smells wafted on to the promenade from the beach. Halos of sun tan lotion hovered around deck chairs. On a day with without any breeze, diesel fumes drifted up from the shore to hang in plumes above the beach.

Don't get me wrong it was a happy place to be. Those who groaned about work, the boss, their football team—on the beach became jovial, talkative, friendly, proffered racing tips and asked you questions from their crossword puzzle book or lap top.

'Want you to go back up Phil,' Bill said as I entered the beach office after housing the trailer.

'Sign out number five machine – take a ticket roll and twenty – five-pound float. Dave's not turned in on the Downs. They'll be thinking them chairs are free with the sunshine – if there's no one about 'til ten.'

'Sure,' I said going over to fetch the ticket machine. I didn't mind working the Downs. A pleasant work station, usually with a bit of a breeze and when not selling tickets sun shaded by the palms dotted across the brown grass.

'You can have your forty-minute break up there and wrap up at five o'clock,' said Bill.

'Okay, that sounds cool,' I said. It suited me fine. I could stack most of the chairs as they left for tea. Hand in the takings at the beach railway office and not have to clear away the chairs on the beach. There were two stacks on the downs and Dan said it usually cleared by five fifteen.

In the carriage going up there was a grey-haired couple with rolled towels under their arms returning, I imagined from a morning swim. At the top a queue tailed around on to the path leading to the ticket office.

Bill was correct in saying that people would think the chairs were free. The grass was covered with the coloured striped chairs. Several couples stood up and walked away as I approached. One circle stayed put.

'We work at the hotel behind.' The dark -haired lad jerked his thumb behind him as if this qualified for free chair usage.

'There are no concessions,' I said.

An attractive red-haired girl in a black mini skirt

girl in a black mini skirt and white top, screwed up her face. 'Bet you've no girl friends with an attitude like that,' she said. Her pony tail switched back and forth, from a determined head flick. Appealing before she opened her mouth. I might have been put out but a date with Pamela, cancelled that out.

If this red-haired bombshell wanted me to feel dejected I didn't. One by one the five of them stood up and sat on the grass. The girl made a point of pulling her skirt down round her thighs as she sat down, to endorse her feelings about my "attitude" as she put it. Holidaymakers though, were in good spirits. One, gave me Dusty Maiden as a sure winner, for the four o'clock at Upton races. I walked back through the scattered clumps of chairs and collected payment from new arrivals.

In the centre of the Downs a circle of chairs was set up. Dan, said The Salvation Army held a Friday sing along. A young woman Salvationist appeared from behind the stack with a chair in each hand.

'It's all right, isn't it?' she said. 'That I prepare the chairs around the band.' A drum thumped from the van on the other side of the road. Caused by a tap from a bandsman. A few holiday-makers were already sat expectantly in chairs.

'The other attendant takes for the chairs just before we start.'

'That's fine,' I said. 'What about your collection doesn't the

fact that they paid once for the chairs put them off donating?'
I asked. She smiled

'It's voluntary no one has to give.'

Opportunities for dates with girls then did seem to surface just, a reminder of what you could be missing. Perhaps, the red-haired girl was into a bit of reverse psychology suggesting I had not got a girlfriend. Maybe, though, she was keen on Dan and disappointed he wasn't in attendance today—who knows? The mind can go on stupid excursions about "what ifs," which are divorced from day-to-day reality, especially when it's to do with girl, boy relationship. I walked across to the balcony overlooking the cliffs, and met with resistance from some punters.

'I didn't expect to pay for the day,' was one try on, as if you could get a reduced ticket – priced for ten minutes – while reading the paper.

'It's an all-day ticket like the car park. You can use the ticket on the beach. Anywhere you go today.' Those who grumbled usually paid up. It was a bit cruel for those with their own car chairs – but that was the ruling, if you sat in a chair, you required a ticket.

'That's my instructions,' I would reply to their look of disbelief. There was a danger of developing the persona of a job's worth. I climbed the steps to the balcony and heard Irish voices. A long dark-haired girl with blue eyes turned to call across.

'Will you be a charging us then? We're working lasses, like you.' Her friend giggled– 'Not a lass, Bernie.' She placed her hand across her mouth to stifle the giggle.

'He's a job to do,' she said and reached across with a pound coin for payment.

'Three please.' I would have paid myself; she was so contrastingly pleasant.

'Where're you working then?' I asked.

'The Belle Vue' she said smiling continuously, which suggested to me at the time that she wouldn't've said no, if I had asked her out – but that's how it goes.

'See you,' she said as I turned to leave. I looked across from the balcony and the Salvationist chairs were now filled. The band set up in the centre with their own folding seats, which were not charged for as Dave said previously. I walked over. An occasional purp came from the brass section. The young Salvationist chatted to holidaymakers. I walked across to the circle of chairs.

'Just in time,' she said as I started issuing tickets. The band started playing – 'What A friend we have in Jesus,' as I issued tickets. The young Salvationist was the soloist. When she started singing everyone stopped talking, evidently captivated by her voice. A breeze lifted the spikes of the palm leaves and some visitors stopped to stand outside the circle to watch and listen. Once I'd collected ticket money from end to end, I walked another round of the Downs. Busy, until three and then it tailed away. A rapid bell ring from the ice cream man encouraged a number out of their chairs. This began a general exodus from chairs.

I cashed up, and put the takings into a zip wallet. Handed it in at the rail ticket office, while fast forwarding my thoughts to my date with Pamela. The chairs stacked like feathers that evening.

Chapter 8

I ASSUMED PAMELA BOARDED at the hotel. Compensation for a lower wage could be that you were given a room with a bed. It might mean sharing, but seaside holiday work was an opportunity to escape from city life or study. My 2008 Vauxhall Astra was parked outside the flat. A prior purchase to leaving the bank. The body work needed attention, but with sixty thousand miles on the clock it still ran well. Perhaps subconsciously bought with a view to changing my life path. There was no real need for a car when buses ran past the house in Grove Green on the outskirts of London, but the Astra became the escape vehicle from my former life.

I'd bought a pasty and cake from the café on the Downs, which I washed down with a mug of tea before getting ready to go out. I decided on a blue jacket, casual shoes and, a smart pair of jeans. The blue jacket. I admit I wanted to make the impression that I had tried to tidy myself up.

The engine kicked into life immediately. A positive omen. The fuel gauge registered quarter full. I was three streets down and drove to Victoria Avenue, adjacent to the hotel. I walked along the front and leant on the high wall outside the hotel. It was seven o'clock. I caught sight of Pamela walking towards me. She was wearing a long woollen cream coat cardigan over a light summer dress – a blue and pink floral clasp holding her hair back on the left side. I stepped away from the wall and she smiled in recognition. I raised my hand, feigning casualness although inwardly thrilled to see her. The evening sun ran along the path behind me and highlighted her dress flicking back and forth as she quickened her pace.

'Hi, I expected you to come out of the hotel,' I said.

'I don't live there. I share a flat with my mother.'

'Oh, right. I somehow imagined you lived in. That makes you local then.

'No, not exactly but where is the car Phil-ip?' 'It's around the corner.'

'Not far then – that's good. I like these shoes very much, but not to walk in,' she said with a smile. I was sufficiently tuned in to how girls prioritize fashion, over comfort, with selection of footwear – I did not query the logic in wearing shoes, which were obviously painful.

We walked along the path. Pamela as if treading on hot coals with the heels of her red shoes clipping the pavement.

'You look great, I said. Your hair looks great. Different from when at work.' I realized after saying the word different that it probably was not an ideal compliment.

'Only different,' she said. 'I've made a special effort for tonight I'd like you to know,' she said tossing back her hair as if piqued, but then broke into a smile.

'It's easy for a man. You're not so judged by your hair and clothes. No, you asked me Phill-ip about being local. We moved over a month ago. We are local and live here now, but— new local.

We turned into Victoria Avenue. The leaves on the Horse Chestnut were sending out suckers that reached across the path.

'That car,' she pointed. It was a convertible BMW soft top. 'No 'fraid not. That one.' I pointed up ahead.

'I like that colour for a car,' she said, straightaway, as if to remedy what might have come across as disappointment.

'It matches my dress – see.' Pamela unbuttoned the cardigan's middle button and opened it in a similar way to a fashion model, who reaches the end of the catwalk. She posed like a model when turned towards me.

'Don't you think Phil-ip? They're a similar shade of green. 'Yes, they are,' I said. My mind was absorbed more with the figure revealed beneath the dress than its colour.

'Yes, that's a coincidence,' I said again. Pamela was stood on the pavement by the bonnet. The Astra was best described as smudgy emerald green. This merged into the green of the hedges and trees. Not really the best colour for leafy country roads in summer. Pamela was way more cultured than most girls that I might meet at the seaside and I wanted to make a good impression. I now felt that the car was not so much an issue, after it got approval for matching the colour of Pamela's mini dress. I pressed the key fob and the locking mechanism clunked open. The cable stich cardigan spread open across each side of the passenger seat, when she got in. I could not help, but admire her legs. She smiled back and while she clicked the seat belt in to fasten it, I started the engine.

I had already caught the allure of scent, but she was not overly made up. A flicker of annoyance crossed her face and her eyes narrowed before she continued.

'My father says I lack the necessary confidence to drive, but I passed the test first time.'

'Good for you,' I said and 'What does your father do?' I asked.

'He's in business, but isn't here now,' she replied.

'What do you do, Phill-ip?' she asked. 'I mean you've not always been a deck chair attendant, have you?' I turned right and approached the main road away from the Downs.

'I was a self-employed artist,' I said, – 'But the cliff path got blocked with rocks.'

'You really paint?' she said sounding impressed.

'I try to, but I was just pencil-sketching portraits.'

'Perhaps you could draw me?' she suggested, as I drove along the front of the Downs.

'I'd love to draw you,' I replied. 'It's five pounds.'

'You'd charge me then Phil-ip?' She looked accusingly across. I smiled before replying.

'No. I'm only joking. I just do a pencil sketch to get the facial look. They're usually quite happy, the visitors that is.'

'Sometimes they just want their dog sketching.'

'That's clever, having a talent, like that. It's very enterprising.' I was finding favour with Pamela.

'I've something to tell you Phil-ip,' she said after a moment's silence.

'You're not married with five children, are you?' I asked 'Don't be silly Phil-ip,' she said and slapped my knee more playfully than with force.

'I'm not married or with anyone else. No, but my real name is Meila not Pamela. I changed it to an English name to make it easier here. I wanted to mention this. It's my birth name and I prefer it. It doesn't matter if you still want to call me Pamela, though,' she looked appealingly across.

It is a lovely name – Meila. Why would anyone not like that name? How are you Meila it's nice to meet you.' I reached over, as if to make an imaginary hand shake. We both laughed. The two names did always intermingle in my mind, but it was at that moment, looking back when I must have fallen even more in love. It was perhaps the appealing and trusting look she gave me. There was delight in her eyes when she could see that I did really like the name Meila.

Within half an hour we arrived at the Mill House Farm Pub. The wheels scrunched on newly laid gravel.

'It's really in the country,' she said as we got out of the Astra. I felt things were going well.

'It has a wheel – look,' she said pointing, as we walked on to the crazy paving area leading to what would have been the farm entrance. The wheel was stopped and the evening light caught on the moss, which clung to paddle blades. The wheel looked forlorn and neglected with sections missing from the boxes, which would have caught the water. Virginia creeper covered the front of the pub. I led the way through a porch which led to double doors and into the bar area. A babble of voices came from the far-right corner where a darts match was in progress. Meila's face lit up.

'This is a real pub,' she said 'not made just for tourists.' Horse brasses, warming pans, pictures of mail coaches on the walls and black oak beams gave it that authentic look.

'They'll welcome tourists all the same,' I said. 'It was a farmhouse. It has still got bags of character.'

'It's really alive in here Phil-ip, Isn't it?'

'You like it then,' I said. There was a spare window seat. 'Shall we sit there,' I pointed across towards it.

'I'd like a Coca Cola with lemon and ice please Phil-ip and you should have a small drink, because you drive.' She was already straightening me out without being asked. Dark eyes flashed that determined look, followed through with that entrapping smile, attractive women can zap you with, knowing they will get their way.

Chapter 9

'YEAH,' CAME FROM THE opposite end where the darts match was in progress. I watched as a slim fair -haired girl, in skin tight jeans reached to take the of double tops, before being lifted into the air by two of her team members. They caught her under the arms and she pumped her legs up and down. The dexterity of the process suggested the ritual was well practiced. I looked back to see Meila standing away from the wall seat to see what was happening. She was smiling and enjoying the spectacle.

The bar girl was serving at the other end, while I watched the darts. I didn't mind Meila reminding me about not to drink and drive. Flattered, that she showed concern for me.

There is always this ambiguous play where the man seeks to please. The woman interested, but then you're still on approval like a set of stamps from Stanley Gibbons that can be returned and forgotten about. We had chatted at the hotel— but it was after all only a first date. I walked across to the bar once the bar girl finished serving at the other end.

'Crisps, get some crisps Phil-ip. I've not had anything to eat since lunch.' I was about to order drinks. The bar girl with an intrigued look on her face. I answered Meila.

'Why didn't you say?' We can probably eat here, Meila,' I said, although I wasn't anticipating forking out for a meal.

'No, No I don't eat in the evenings now. She made as if to position the top with her hands. My appreciative look made her smile.

'I must stay on my diet. Then I will decide afterwards if I'm suitable for bikini wearing on the beach.' There was no doubt in my mind on that score whether she dieted or not.

'I'll have hot chilli-flavour, if they have them or just plain,' Meila said. The bar girl reached down and produced a packet of chilli crisps.

'Your wife's in luck,' she said. The conversation somehow implying that we were married. I sort of mumbled a reply. What do you say? That we weren't married. That this was a first date?

'Great,' I said. 'A coke with lemon and a half of Butcombe bitter as well, please.'

'Will your wife be wanting ice?'

'Yes, and the young woman with me is not my wife.' 'Sorry, I got that wrong then. There was I thinking you'd be wanting a room.' Her eyes gave out a forward meaning appreciation, which I could have done without as the Coke frothed into the glass from the tap. She moved away, but cheekily looked back and said-

'Perhaps you will?' In her twenties and not unattractive. She didn't wait for an answer, but smiled, digging the tongs into an ice bucket, obviously amused at her own narrative, regarding my relationship with Meila.

The noise from the darts match, hopefully, meant that Meila couldn't hear, and the teams were already drifting over to my side of the bar.

'You're driving the mini bus Jack,' a tall ginger bearded lad in a rugby shirt called out. I'll get you a soft drink, seeing as you're on the wagon tonight.'

'Yes, Jack's not to drink,' the fair-haired girl called out. 'Jack's not to drink, Jack's not to drink,' they chorused.

'All right, all right, I get the message,' said Jack standing at the back.

'That'll be seven-fifty,' said the girl, placing the drinks and crisps on a tin tray. I extricated myself from the crowd glad that I had been ahead of the darts teams.

'That's something I'd like,' said Meila, 'to be in a darts team.' 'Do you mean that?' I said placing the tray on the table and passing over the crisps and coke.

'They had a darts team at Uni, but it was all boys. I would prefer there to be a mix, but more boys than girls,' she said smiling mischievously. The two teams in the pub met her criteria. Two girls and the fair haired one in what looked like two teams of six players. I took a sip of my beer.

'So. what are you doing here?' I asked making conversation.

'Because you brought me Phil-ip,' she replied with a serious face, before laughing. I'm sure she knew what I meant.

'I meant working at Sea View.'

'My father's travelling in business. My mother, said living in the city was too much like Hong Kong, with the air pollution and wanted to move to the seaside for the fresh air.'

'You mean London?' 'Yes London.'

'A man who is tired of London is tired of life.' – I quoted Samuel Johnson's famous observation.

'But my mother is not a man though,' said Pamela – and this is not the eighteenth century.'

'True.' Meila scored a win for women.

'Where were you at Uni?'

'Bristol,' she said, 'I got a 2.1. I read Economics with History.'

'And you have a student type job.'

'You know how long it takes waiting to be called for interview. And then my mother was moving. I didn't want to work in a city office any longer.'

She shrugged her shoulders.

'Or do home type work and not see anyone. Mother is opening a boutique. I might even help her run it, if things get desperate.'

'You could get a well-paid job in the public sector,' I suggested.

'Maybe, but it's the summer and I'm liking the rest preparing for job interviews and the pretence that you're really interested in a company that you researched on the internet a couple of week s ago.' Well-defined eyebrows and dark brown eyes looked captivatingly over the Coke glass as she sipped it.

'Maybe it's the same for you? Meila continued. 'You haven't always been a painter...have you Phill-ip?'

'No, but art was my choice of course at college. But I ended up working at a bank. I gave in my notice in February. Just packed my belongings in the Astra and moved down here.

'That was very courageous to do that.'

'Do you really think so? Courageous or foolish depends how you look at it,' I said.

'I didn't have a job to go to.'

'But you were doing something you liked.'

'I was—before the rock fall – well I still am, I enjoy working on the beach and the Downs and I wouldn't have met you at the Sea View.' Her eyelids fluttered, seemingly pleased that I said that. A couple walked by and sat at the table next to the fireplace.

'I'll have a white wine, that'll do Andy.' The woman said, looking to check her face in a warming pan on the wall before sitting down. Her brusque manner suggesting all was not well.

'They've had a row,' said Pamela.

'How can you tell?'

'The way she went to sit down without looking at him when she talked. They look as if they're trying to make up.' I couldn't see this, but as a man, perhaps I did not possess Meila's intuitive reasoning. I surprised myself, then with my direct approach to planning another date, when I said,

'They're having a beach party on Saturday. Would you like to come?' It seemed like an opportunity to get another date.

'Maybe, will you be playing darts?'

'No, but I could set up a dart board on a tree or something,' I said.

'I was only joking,' she said, running her fingers through her hair.

'Perhaps, we could return to the Downs,' she said. For one perilous moment I thought my date with Meila was unravelling.

'Have you got an early start tomorrow, I mean –

'No, Phill-ip,' she said, nodding her head from side to side, with a mischievous smile

'But there's The Blue Comet. Do you know it?'

'Yes, of course,' I said. 'I know it, but I'm not a member.' 'They'll let me in, with you.'

'Because you're, a girl. 'Maybe,' she said casually.

'Sounds okay to me. I can park nearby and we're in walking distance of where we both live.'

'Do you drink, a lot then Phill-ip?' she asked. 'No but it's easy to go over the limit.'

'You were here with that girl from work,' I caught the conversation from the next table.

'No.'

'I saw you.

'You've been spying on me Angie,' the man said

'I don't want to listen in on that,' I said to Meila. 'Good time to leave.'

Chapter 10

I PARKED THE ASTRA outside my flat, but decided not to tell Pamela I lived there. Yes, I was embarrassed about the state of it and decided that it needed tidying up before I asked her back. It was the next date that focused my attention. There'd been a maybe to the beach party before the Blue Comet night club was suggested. Attraction from the boy sees girl and likes what he sees to the boy wants to meet girl again because she's even more attractive than the imaginary construct pre-going out. I was now tangled in hopeful anticipation that she would say yes to another date.

Meila wasn't every day for me. I knew this when I first went to the reception desk with the invoice to authorize. Pleased with myself for getting up courage to ask her out. The waitress on the downs and the Salvation Army girl, would still be there. Arrogance slipped into the equation. I pretended to myself that meeting Meila was just a holiday happening, but I knew really this wasn't true. She stopped walking – put a hand against the wall and kicked off her shoes – grabbed them by the straps and walked barefoot along the path leading back to the Downs.

'That's better. It'll break my feet in for walking bare foot at the beach party,' she said. That remark went through my body like a warm embrace. I reached to touch her arm. She turned and smiled. We held hands. It was a faster pace than before. Pamela's feet sprung from the path like a trained dancer's. My concerns about a future date evaporating. Spirits lifted by her remark about the beach party.

The Blue Comet was three doors down from Sea View. Set back from the road with pillars supporting jagged white chains above a graveled forecourt. A wooden canopied veranda for serving teas and coffees. The sun brollies furled. Backs of chairs pulled up against the tables for the night. The

45

electrified writing – *Blue Comet* – on the wall above flickering on and off.

'I like the way you say my name,' I said as Pamela stopped outside to put on her shoes. She placed a hand on my shoulder.

'But it's your name – Phil-ip,' she said.

'Yes, but not everyone says it that way. They usually call me Phil.'

'Don't you think it's okay to be Phil-ip.' She said giving a disappointed look, letting go of my hand.

'No, no, quite the opposite, I like it,' 'But then I like your name Meila.'

'Not Pamela?'

'Yes, both names—they're both you to me,' I said. 'But Meila's the name you like the most and so do I.'

I wanted to kiss in the car park, but it was noisy with car doors slamming. We stepped across to the veranda, but Meila stopped and turned. Her hand reached to my shoulder and she kissed my cheek in the fading light. My hands encircled her waist and she wrapped her arms around me. The unbuttoned cardigan meant Meila's firm breasts rested against me. Neither of us sought to advance the kiss into a French kiss. It must have been about five seconds that we held each other, but it was over too quickly for me. Pent up feelings of attraction met. Meila, drew away and held my hands before saying.

'We'd better go inside Phill-ip, don't you think?'

'Okay,' I said and we smiled at each other. After leaving the Mill Farm pub I wasn't sure how it was going, but a feeling of uncertainty was replaced by one of happy acceptance; now that we'd kissed and held each other. We were no longer trying to read how we felt about each other. We entwined arms and walked towards the double door entrance. One was open. A door man in a dark suit and white gloves opened the other.

'Good evening, Miss Evans. You are accepting our invitation to visit.'

'Yes, I've brought my boyfriend, if that's all right?' I was

Meila's boyfriend. Did I really hear that said!

'That's perfectly all right. You are both welcome.'

There was a wide hall entrance and a stairway at the back with rooms leading off.

I discovered later that the Blue Comet night club was a conversion from a hotel. The ground floor given over to a selection of bars, but the main dining area and guest room knocked through to form a dance floor.

'How do you get in free?' I asked as Pamela handed over her long cardigan at the cloak room. The pastry chef at Sea View supplies cakes and pies for the cafeteria in the day time. I must take the cheque payment every Friday and give a receipt. They say I can go there in the evening for free, anytime I want.'

I knew they let girls in free to boost the appeal of a club. I wasn't that surprised.

'I asked if I could bring a friend. I would never come on my own,' she said taking the ticket as the girl safety pinned the duplicate to the cardigan.

'You're a frequent visitor then, I said.

'No, not frequent. Olga, she has been here with me. You are the first boy.'

'And who's Olga?'

'A waitress at the hotel. Why do you ask?' 'Just curious that's all.'

A bass guitar strummed. The sound came from the doors on the left, which opened as a couple came out releasing a babble of voices from within.

'I like the Oyster Bar,' said Pamela as I followed her across to the far side. Through an entrance with the door removed to open a view of the inside bar. A bar man, in a white coat put down a silver cocktail shaker and greeted Pamela as we entered.

'Buenos noches senorita Pamela. It is good to see you here and you're not working. That is tres bueno.' 'Hello Pedro,' said Pamela. What's that?'

47

'You like cocktail. Pedro is mixing a Spanish Pampero. It is a new one I make. It has a fiery temperament.'

'No, that'll give me a headache. I'll stick with a pineapple squash, thanks.'

'And your friend?' Pedro turned to me, but I sensed that he would have preferred to have had Pamela to himself, although it must have been apparent that we were very much together. There was a tall refrigerator behind with various beers and lagers.

'I'll have a lager Pedro,' I said. He turned away to prepare the drinks.

'You like it.'

'It is cosy in here.

'I prefer it to the larger bars.'

'You're definitely the pearl in the oyster bar then,' I said. 'You say that, and perhaps you really mean it?' she smiled.

Her face was flushed, probably like mine after the embrace and kiss on the veranda

'I wouldn't' — I was interrupted by Pedro speaking.

'You are not here to collect money for the hotel – I have to charge you,' said Pedro, turning to break the cap off the lager bottle from under the bar.

'That's all right I'll pay,' I said. Pedro moved away to get ice for the squash.

'No, this time I pay Phill-ip. You're working in a holiday job. I'd like to buy a drink for the chauffeur, she said, and smiled at me. Pedro heard the mention of the word chauffeur, but evidently not that we both worked in a holiday job.

'You are special person tonight with a chauffeur senorita Pamela, then,' he said.

'Yes, I am.' Pedro took the word chauffeur literally when it was just a remark you make when someone does the driving on a night out.

When we left the bar, she said,

'Let's go over there. As far away from here, as possible,

48

Pedro gives me the creeps. He smiles all the time, but his eyes are cold and lifeless.

'He seemed friendly enough,' I said. Too friendly, but I never said that to Meila.

'I have to start work at eight thirty tomorrow. You don't mind if we have just the one drink.'

'No, that's okay. The beach party, next Friday—shall I meet you again at the hotel?'

'Yes, but who else will be there?' When Meila spoke her lips were even more inviting now that we'd kissed.

'People like me, who work on the beach, mainly,' I said. Ice clinked in the glass as she took a sip.

'That's okay. But it's girls, not just your friends from work.'

'I do have friends, who are girls.'

'But not a girlfriend, that I share with?'

'No, of course not,' I said.

We left after half an hour. That Meila wanted to have an early night worked out okay.

It avoided her meeting up with my dilapidated flat, which I'd decided should remain in the background. Girls I'd discovered were a bit fastidious about the spec of flats.

Mine ticked low spec.

Meila, collected her cardigan from the cloak room and we went out into the warm night air.

'We don't live far from here,' she said.

There were a few couples on the Downs, but no one nearby. We stopped and turned toward each other.

'It's been a nice evening together,' she said. I moved forward and held her waist.

'It's been great Meila – I mean going out with you,' I said. We kissed and she said,

'Look forward to seeing you Phill-ip when you visit the hotel And I'm looking forward to the beach party on Saturday, next week.'

'See you at reception, then.'

'Oh, yes, she said. 'I may never wear these shoes again and bent her knee to remove first one shoe then the other. They sparkled under the street lamp.

'I'll let you know more about the party then.'

Meila waved while in bare feet carrying shoes and handbag.

Chapter 11

'YOU SAY YOU'RE GOING to get a flat. I feel like some school girl getting off behind the bike shed,' said Julie.

'Another fortnight and one will be available. We can meet on my day off. Mary goes to her mothers in the afternoon, it's all coming together Jules.'

'Promises, promises. Terry's going away on conference at the end of August. The flat needs to be sorted by then.'

'I'm working towards that. Aunt Grace's estate is still being wound up by the solicitor, but he can make an interim payment. It'll be enough for a flat. She had property in Spain, but it's taken a while to sell.'

'I've heard all this before.'

'It's true. You seem to think I'm not as keen as you to get together permanently.'

'You've not told Mary?'

'What's the point. She's best kept in the quiet. It'll cause a fuss. I'd rather that came at the end of the season.

'I don't know how Terry will react, but then I'm not bothered,' said Julie. 'He'll not know that he talks about his new PA in his sleep. That it's all become an act on his part even having sex now every Saturday.

'I just hope I don't talk about you when I'm asleep, 'said Bill.

'You don't have dreams about us together then.'

'If I do, I don't remember them, afterwards. I do my dreaming about you all day Julie.'

'Then dream about having a flat and not just rendezvousing in the ticket office then.'

'Look over there there's Dan from the beach,' said Julie.

A young couple stood at the bar

'They're so sweet. Look at the way she's looking at him.

I remember that feeling – being with the best -looking guy

in the room when I was about eighteen. The girl flicked her hair back, and smiled.

'Yes, sweetheart you've got the best catch in the room.'

'You're not after a toy boy are you, Jules?'

'Don't be daft Bill, he'd be more interested in my bank account and what it can buy than anything else. No, she believes she has got the goods. At her age I'd have been the same. You go after a man to show off with and Dan fits that bill.'

'And there was I thinking that's exactly what a man does when he goes after a girl,' said Bill. Dan caught sight of the two of them sat in the corner of the bar and waved. Julie waved back and smiled, Bill lifted his beer glass a couple of times, in recognition of Dan's catch, while the fair-haired girl was pretending not to notice them.

'I've got these from the estate agents.' Julie produced a sheaf of property brochures from her beach bag.

'You're previous with those,' said Bill. 'Anyway, it's better to look at estate agents flats websites these days. The information's likely to be more up to date. I've got somewhere in mind.'

'I don't want you making the decision on your own,' said Julie.

'Look this one's got a balcony and a shared garden,' Julie pointed at a white block with palm trees in the front with an additional view of the sweep of the road along the front. I'd like to look at that one. We could go to look on your day off.'

'Can't this week. I've got an appointment with John at the Sea View. He wants to up the delivery of dairy products from the ferry for next month.

'And you're going on your day off?'

'We can meet up afterwards.' Bill taking a long drink from his beer mug before continuing with

'Maybe.'

'I asked Phil that new attendant if he'd sketch me holding Buggles.'

'That dog's totally spoilt. You're not having him sketching you in the ticket office.'

'I might. I've always fancied being an artist's model. Getting paid for having a man look at you from behind an easel is preferable to being gawped at as a sort of unpaid sex object.'

'You know I'm not like that,' said Bill moving closer to Julia in the window seat and placing his arm around her shoulder to gently caress her cheek and neck. Julie turned towards him.

'I never said you were, did I?'

Chapter 12

'SPECIALITY CHIPS, WHOEVER HEARD of such a thing?' They're just chips dropped in cheese batter mix. How ridiculous,' said Rita, Pamela's, mother.

'They batter Mars bars and crème eggs if you ask.' 'I do hope you've not been eating them, Pamela.'

'I might,' she said. Pamela liked to confound her mother's aspirations.

Rita's, first name in Hong Kong was Ling, but where Pamela liked close friends to call her Meila Rita, never wanted to keep the name Ling. She was Rita Tomkins, A dress designer in the Hong Kong department store, when Alex, first asked her out. She was Rita, to her customers and senior management even then.

The corner restaurant, below the flat did "take away food." Not Rita's, idea of good living, but the flat was useful as a hideaway. It was far removed from the apartment in Piccadilly. The entrance down an alley at the back of the restaurant. The removal of the gate meant there was no number to show the flat existed. Deliveries were taken in by t restaurant when open. The restaurant owner let the upstairs flat after an online enquiry by Rita.

The small back bedroom had been turned into a kitchen next to the former main bedroom, now the lounge. A corridor led to Rita's bedroom and a second smaller one, further down which Pamela occupied.

Pamela sat on the settee in a pink bathrobe after showering. She'd attended to all messages on her Smartphone. She picked up the hand mirror from the floor and placed it on the coffee table. A circular mirror, which rotated to a side with magnification. This allowed for better inspection of freckles, that needed to be hidden from public gaze. Her mother walked in from the kitchen and placed a tray next to the coffee percolator.

'Did you have a nice night, Pamela?' Was he worth all the preparation?'

'How do you know I went out with a boy last night?' What if I said I went out with Olga the waitress.'

'Then you'd be lying. No woman spends time with her hair like you did last night unless of course you have a feminist girlfriend.

'No mother feminists don't necessarily sleep with other women.'

Pamela stopped talking to extricate the hair brush from the tangle in her hair.

'You're just fishing. He's sweet and friendly and I think a bit lonely.'

'He's not from around here. Like you then?'

'Perhaps.' Pamela felt a warm glow remembering the night before.

'He works on the beach as an attendant. I first saw him on the Downs from the hotel window.'

'A beach bum Pamela. Just a beach bum and you went out with him!'

'He'll not be able to keep you in nice house and support family.' Unlike Pamela, who grew up in England, Rita's English could lapse when she became excited.

'How can you say that mother?'

'Here's a coffee and you should eat something.' Her mother placed a breakfast sized cup of coffee on the table next to the settee.

'We're working for the Summer. He's, like me, taking a rest from more serious work,' Pamela said while she dabbed cream on newly discovered cheek freckles.

'Money's not everything.'

'It's important to live well, though – your father has bought a farm out on Dartmoor. It's not in his name.

It has backing from a charity that gives not so well children horse riding and farm experience.

'Really? I don't see father as a farmer.'

'He'll be – he says off grid. Now, your father has a property and share in that night club – not just a Range Rover full of gold bars.'

'You could be a celebrity in the community. There can't be many Asian farmer's wives about.'

'No that is not the intention. It's intended as a smoke screen. I'm still planning to find a shop for a dress boutique – and you can help me look Pamela.'

'I may help you look, but I'm not standing in your shop all day.'

'You need to be occupied. Your father only wants you to be at the hotel for the summer and then what will you do?' Pamela popped bread in the toaster and sat down again to continue getting her face and hair ready for work. This included a close inspection of the extent of eyebrow growth, which Pamela referred to as her eye brow moustaches.

'You say that as if I have no qualifications and will be lucky if someone employs me outside the family. This is temporary and I said to father that I would help out. When I go to the Blue Comet and they just think I'm the girl who works at the hotel.'

'It is better that way. To be like others is how your father keeps safe. The cruise ships will soon be finished and then it will be quiet and safer for us all.'

'And you're going to live on the farm?'

'No. I will live where my boutique is. Your father knows this. The farm will be managed by the charity. An electronic bell like beep came from Pamela's Smartphone.

'Is that the time?' Pamela picked up her coffee and went to her bedroom, leaving the door open. Toast popped.

'What are you having on this toast Pamela?' called out her mother.

'Peanut butter thinly spread with strawberry jam – and cut into squares,' said Pamela.

'Yes, my lady – ugh! I can't understand how you can eat such rubbish.' Pamela chose not to hear. Rita prepared the plate of toast and took it in to Pamela's bedroom, placing it next to the coffee on the bedside table. Pamela, having removed her dressing gown was stood, in front of the wardrobe mirror in bra and briefs, to inspect her nearly flat stomach.

'There's nothing there Pamela.'

'I'll be the judge of that,' she said, having already decided on eating only one square of peanut butter and jam toast.

I'm going to a beach party, mother next Saturday week.'

'With that same young man.'

'No, the man in the Moon.'

'It is perhaps not so bad getting to know someone from the beach. What did you say his name was?' Her mother partly opened the bedroom windows to let in more light before she sat on Pamela's bed. Pamela removed from her wardrobe, a short –sleeved halter necked blue dress with a black velvet bow.

'I didn't,' she said, and held the dress against her. Phill-ip, would she considered probably prefer to see her in a revealing dress, than something more formal when he visited Sea View. She would wear the dress today, Sunday, and then again on Tuesday when he visited to have the invoice stamped.

'Phill-ip,' she said, as much to please herself with speaking his name than to inform her mother.

'That is not too bad a name,' Rita said, without giving it much attention.

'Your father pays that inspector very well to make sure the cool boxes are delivered safely and not tampered with.'

'He knows what's in them then? Asked Pamela.

'No, of course not. He believes they contain mainly dairy product, but some duty free. Cigarettes, whisky and gin. That is the secret. Cocaine, and some knew chemical drugs are being brought ashore, but no duty free. It is funny how smuggled duty free is something that many people see as all right.'

57

Pamela twirled in front of the mirror to gauge whether the dress settled where she wanted it on her legs.

'Phil-ip, delivers these boxes to the hotel from the beach.

'That is how I met him.'

'Be careful Pamela, your father may not like this to continue as a friendship for you. He may think he will discover, who you really are.' Pamela did not mention that she'd told Phillip her birth name, knowing her mother would not like that.

'I'm never going to talk about father or about the business. Do you think I'm stupid?'

'No Pamela, but you like this boy – no?'

'Like, because he is friendly and interesting. I need to be with my generation. It doesn't mean that it may go any further than just friendship.' It had but, Meila chose not to tell her mother. He's an artist and was getting paid to sketch visitors walking to and from the beach, but now the path is blocked by fallen rocks. You see he is resourceful mother.'

'An artist. He probably wants to sketch you in the nude. To get you undressed, and make love in the name of art. You with a good degree and then I have a daughter who wants only to sell her body.'

'You shouldn't give me ideas like that mother. I've only been out with him once.'

Her mother got up and went back to the sitting room to switch on the radio.

'What did you say, mother?' Rita raised her voice over the local traffic news.

'You need to hurry up or you'll be late for work.'

Chapter 13

THERE WAS A DRUM roll followed by some talking from the theatre. The gardener's hut was built on the remaining space before the precipitous cliffs took over. The theatre seated three hundred and was at the end of the Downs. It provided entertainment through the summer. The performers not well known, but sought to find an enthusiastic audience from the tourists staying nearby.

The hut was like a base camp, where the day started and ended. Dan's ticket machine, the flapped leather shoulder bag for coins, notes, spare ticket rolls and the takings book were kept in a cupboard on the back wall. The takings were listed for the day and handed in with the cash at either the theatre or rail ticket office.

A selection of rakes, hoes, spades, forks, and half-moon shaped turf cutters were held by pairs of nails, which when removed left a dark impression on the wood, due to the sun bleaching the surrounding wood varnish.

Knowing that I would return here I'd left pencils, coloured chalks a box of charcoal, sketch pads A6 up to A3 plus a folding easel stand at the back of the cupboard.

My deck chair attending day ended at five-thirty. There was still quite good light and the idea was to perhaps catch a few theatre goers who'd arrived early. I was chatting to Dan in the morning on the promenade. He'd chosen to visit the beach on his day off.

'Are you that hard up Phil that you have to work after hours,' he said.

For Dan any activity other than downing a few tinnies or going to a Barbie was interpreted as work.

'I find it relaxing and people are happy when they're on holiday. They don't expect a Michaelangelo standard piece of art. It's not easy to explain but it gives me space to unwind.'

This took place when we were standing on the promenade earlier. I wasn't sure Dan was convinced by my answer, but it was then that Dan dropped the bombshell about the beach party Saturday week when he said.

'I've got to get a Barbie together for the beach party on Thanet Island. I'm seeing if Ingrid can help with paper cups and plates. That's why I'm down here today, he said.

'Thanet Island?' I exclaimed. This was the craggy clump of rock several hundred yards out to sea.

'Yep, Phil – didn't I say the beach parties on the island. It's got a sandy beach around the back. It's just the ticket for a party. When the tides out that is. Mal's letting us have Sea Spray to get out there.'

'You didn't tell me.'

'Well, you know now, so that's okay.' It wasn't okay, because Meila must have presumed the party was on Babbacombe Beach. Now, I would need to do some explaining.

What if she couldn't swim or was scared of boats? It was Sunday and somehow Dan had wangled the day off. I was now his regular stand in on the Downs so I would be able to see her. In one sense I couldn't have asked for a better arrangement. In particular, only the day after and I would be able to se Meila or as I needed to remember that she was Pamela to the outside world.

Tuesday and Fridays were often delivery days for the cool boxes. The weekend was a busy time for cream teas. Sea View prepared baked trays of apple pie for delivery to the café on the downs. The Spanish chef liked to deliver these personally to the cafe owner. After the first day visitors tended to have put aside the right money. Today, for obvious reasons I'd decided to visit the hotel for one and fifty pence coins. The other option was dropping in on Mrs Brown at the Red and White rose café half way along on the other side of the Downs road.

"The receptionist at the Sea View will give you coins

usually, but they don't like riff raff like us in the foyer in the morning. Only go in the mid-afternoon." Those were Dan's words about getting change for the cash satchel. The takings went in a zip leather wallet, but a twenty-five-pound float was held back for the following day. It needed to contain ten, fifty, and twenty pence coins with a smattering of smaller ones.

My mind wandered through about what I'd say to Meila that afternoon and whether she'd still want to go to the beach party. I was telling myself, if Meila didn't want to go to the beach party, neither would I.

I normally went to the café and chatted with Mrs Brown. Listened to how her daughter was struggling in the world of work and how much her horse cost to feed. She recruited us as ambassadors.

'Do tell them about the café. There's a charge for the tray of two it's refundable. We've a café room upstairs tell them. Just because it's full downstairs when it's raining – I've still got room. She made her café sound like a bomb shelter from attacks by the enemy. The enemy being in this instance the rain, although she was proud that her mother's tea house in the East End was the only one that stayed open during the London Blitz.

Her daughter Zoe helped out, with her partner when it was sunny and busy, but when the rain swirled across the downs she managed on her own – still full then with visitors killing time with the hope that the rain would stop. On a sunny day the Downs became exceptionally busy. It's not necessarily true that everyone preferred the beach. Family groups enjoyed the sea. There was a water ski school, a speed boat, pedalos,' row boats and a diving board, easily accessible when the tide was out.

The sun beat down and reflected heat from the pebbles. You could get a sensation of frying when sat in a deck chair. Couples on their own and older people holidaying there for the week resisted the allure of the beach and would sit overlooking the bay. A gentle breeze today helped reduce the sun's intensity.

'On Safari then?' I turned to see a couple I'd not seen before. I'd borrowed one of Dan's Aussie Bush type hats. The man was wearing a Panama hat. I resisted asking if he thought he was on a liner going through Panama, but 'It gets warm enough at times to make you think you're in another country. The only shooting around here is when they have a target range at the fairground

'When's that?' he asked.

'At the season end. Not for over a month, but I'm told the show at the music hall is quite entertaining. Two chairs, that'll be fifty pence, please.'

He stood up from the chair and produced his wallet from his back pocket, handing me a five -pound note Visitors asked about the local attractions and I generally put a positive spin on what was on offer.

'I'd like to go to that,' the woman, said. 'The evening show, that is.'

'You'd best book. There's only seating for three hundred. The booking office is open from midday until five.' I pointed across to the pathway at the end – the theatre obscured by rockery and palm trees.

'Thank you,' she reached up to take the tickets from me and took the change.

'Hey, that was sneaky,' he said.

'I'll be wanting an ice cream and you'll most likely be asleep Chris.'

He threw up his hands in mock despair, sat down again, but didn't seem to mind. The sun was shining, he was relaxed and friendly to the world, including his wife.

A balcony was situated about halfway along the downs. There was a slope on the grass which led to the concrete path that almost made you start running. I jumped over the green hoops that protected flower beds, while I held the money pouch to stop coins jumping out. A couple were taking turns to look through the pay view telescope next to the green bench by the balcony. This was when I first met Maria.

I recognized the group of four Irish girls, who were sat in the balcony, as before. Two were in waitress uniforms and two in dresses. This was where I first met Maria, who was sat at the far end of the row of chairs. The two waitresses in black dresses, without their aprons stood up immediately when I climbed the steps to the balcony. One of them the red haired one I'd met before. The other with long black hair pinned up. I asked for their tickets knowing full well they hadn't any. It was unlikely that they'd been on the beach to buy them. It was Maria, who I'd not met before, who said she'd pay.

'Do you mean that Maria?' said the girl sat next to her. 'Yes, if you say you can share the flat with me, of course I'll pay. How much is it?' She asked turning towards me as I walked across the concrete floor of the balcony. A warm breeze scooted through the chairs, which lifted the plastic fabric up.

'It's twenty-five pence for the day. You can take the ticket on to any beach.

'Where's Dan,' she asked.

'I'm sorry to disappoint you, but it's Dan's day off.' She reached down to get her purse out of her handbag inside a straw beach bag, while turning to her friend.

'There you are, he told me he worked every day on the Downs after helping on the beach and it's his day off—would you believe it.'

'Well Maria, he would 've been working, anyway' said the girl sitting next to her. I reckoned Maria was in her late twenties. Long black hair with the occasional white strand. Pale blue eyes with sunglasses perched on her forehead. Crossed mini-skirted legs, with that sheen from genuine sun tan. I could see the appeal for Dan.

'You'll embarrass him,' said the dark-haired waitress, who seemed more on my side than the red haired one.

'I never even knew you'd met Dan, Maria,' she continued. 'He's invited me to go with him to a beach party,' said Maria and handed a pound coin to me.

'Two tickets please' – I gave two turns on the machine.

'I told you, that parties on the beach,' said the red -haired waitress to her friend. Both stood with their backs to the railing to avoid ticket payment. The atmosphere cooled after Maria said she was the one asked by Dan to accompany him. Maria was very friendly. The other three not that pleased to see me. It was deck chair attendant Dan that they'd been waiting for. The waitress who gave me the cold shoulder last time we met, nearly managed a smile as she looked across. Then pursed her lips and looked to one side to exhale cigarette smoke. This time more a re-appraisal type of look, perhaps she sensed I was more at ease. Maybe I appeared more so now that I was dating Meila. I handed Maria the tickets plus the fifty pence change.

'It's on a beach, but not the beach down there. I pointed over the railings and at the white spread of pebbles, now dotted with deck chairs, that was Babbacombe. It's on Thanet island. With a beach on the other side. It's accessible at low tide by boat.

'You know all about it then?' said Maria.

'Not really,' I said. 'I've only recently found out from Dan that the party's on Thanet island.' I decided then not to tell Maria, that I met up with Dan on the beach earlier.

'It sounds fun,' she said and turned to the girl sat next to her and said,

'I've got to see the police about Alfie's belongings later today.'

'Is that right Maria?' she said and got out of the deck chair to get a light from the dark-haired waitress. The lighter was held below the railings to avoid the breeze. I tried to go unnoticed, when I looked at tanned legs when she leant forward to catch a spurting flame from a lighter. The red head was feisty.

All four girls were individually incredibly attractive. But now that I had been out with Meila, there was no contest.

'Alfie, Alfie, the name came back to me.'

'Are you, I mean, were you Alfie's girlfriend.' It was said a bit incredulously and without really thinking. Maria stopped talking to her friend.

'I don't look that old do I?' But she smiled as she said it.

'No Alfie, was my step brother. Did you know him?'

The red-haired girl, interrupted.

'Colleen look at the time. We're supposed to be back for ten. I stood back to let the two waitresses go between us.

Chapter 14

'**Did you know him?**' asked Maria again after the waitresses left to go back to work.

'No, but Dan worked with Alfie on the beach. You should ask him,' I said.

'They all liked Alfie and they said he loved the job. ' 'There you are Maria he died doing what he liked. Not a bad way to go,' said Maria's friend, who remained after other waitresses left to go back to work.

'I suppose so Sal, but he'd never not worked and didn't smoke or drink. He was very fit for his age.'

'I'm so sorry,' I said. I replaced Alfie the following week.'
'There's nothing for you to feel sorry about. Don't be sorry. I'm the one to feel sorry. I was in South Africa for Save The Children. Three weeks later when I returned there were two cops on my doorstep. It was a real shock when they told me about Alfie's death. They said, as far as they knew he'd collapsed, on the beach with a heart attack.

Two visitors found him face down behind a large boulder.'
'This happened when you were in Africa and you didn't know anything about it until much later, though,' said Sally.

'Not only that but he'd been buried. Apparently, all he cut the grass in St Peter's church and reserved himself a burial plot. We had no relatives. Not here anyway. My mother and step– father emigrated to Australia and arranged the burial with the vicar by telephone.'

'I heard he had a good send off,' I said.

'Apparently most of the beach staff attended, And Mrs Brown from the beach café, her daughter, and the manager of the Sea View.'

'But not me,' said Maria. Sally put her arm around Maria. 'You couldn't help that; you shouldn't upset yourself.'

'The clothes he was wearing and some personal belongings

need collecting from the police station. I've seen the solicitor and he's awaiting probate. That's what he told me. They've put Alfie's belongings from the flat into storage and are going to contact me when everything's settled.'

'I'll come with you to the police station, if you'd like me to,' said Sally.

'Will you really – thanks Sal.'

'Dan's looking after Skittles, Alfie's cat,' I said.

'Dan never told me that.'

'Perhaps he just didn't think to say,' said Sally. I remembered Bill telling me this when I first started. Just then I looked up in time to catch sight of the area beach inspector's car turn the corner on to the Downs Road. He might be able to see me from the road. I decided to get a move on.

'I'll see you at the party, then,' I said, departing to sell tickets to an elderly couple sat in the right corner of the balcony. You were not openly discouraged from chatting to people in their deck chairs, but it was all about selling as many tickets as possible, while the sun shone.

'Is the main shopping centre far from here, dearie?' asked the white-haired old lady in glasses.

'We arrived last night. How much is the charge for the chairs did you say?' I hadn't said.

'There's a bus stop on the main road opposite the Downs. It's a fifteen-minute ride to the town centre.' I turned with my back to the sea and pointed to my right.

'Or a ten-minute walk to the local shops. There's a post office a grocers' and a chemist.' After a day in the sun there was a mass exodus to buy sun cream, sun glasses and other paraphernalia.

'The chairs are twenty-five pence. You can stay all day.'

'I don't think we'll be doing that the sun is fierce after midday. What do you think George?'

'Well, yes, dear.' George lowered his book from his eyes and gazed forward vacantly from his chair for a moment.

'You could return in the late afternoon. It does usually cool down by four,' I said, sensing that there was a monumental decision in progress.

'George. Are we staying or not?'

'We can do both. You want to go to the shops. We'll have to buy tickets anyway and we can come back later.' He looked up at me to affirm a sort of male bonding appreciation about shops.

'We can come back here later Martha and make the most of the sun. They won't want us back in the hotel before six.' This seemed to finalize the decision.

'Two tickets, dear,' she smiled and handed me a fifty pence piece. I heard wood sliding against wood as chairs were pulled away from a stack next to the path. Unlike on the beach, visitors to the Downs might help themselves to chairs and set them up on their own accord. I didn't mind. Some would later even fold the chair up and take it back to the stack. When close by I would wave and give a thumbs up. There was always the possibility that Dan had trained his customers up to return the chairs, so he could finish early.

Two hours must have passed with the need to replace the ticket roll in the process, before I looked at the clock face of the church visible at the end of St Peter's Road.

It read twelve twenty-five. With my break due at twelve thirty I left the grass of the Downs and started down the path to the gardener's shed. My lunch was usually of the sandwich variety topped up with a bought apple or peach pie, which were unappetizing unless heated. These I ate outside overlooking the wooded part, which led to the Blackberry Cove just beneath the Downs. Dan said a twelve thirty break was the best time.

I have to admit my mind was occupied with visiting Sea View on the pretext of needing to change coins for notes – when really it was all about seeing Meila with the hope that she wouldn't be put off having to go in a boat. It was one of those what if situations.

What if she said she hated going in boats? That she couldn't swim? That my taking her to the beach party was called off? These considerations crowded my mind as I returned to collect ticket money after my lunch break. There were some empty chairs, but new faces to sell tickets to. Earlier the change situation remained balanced, but true to form the regulars started giving the right amount in coins and they built up. My insecurity level rose when I stopped near to the gate which led into the hotel with an anxiety that it could be Miela's day off. I walked past the fierce looking vulture like birds, which didn't seem to scare the gulls and then through the front entrance, which was a hall corridor. It appeared dark inside compared with the bright sunlight outside. My hopes sunk when as I got accustomed to the light. I couldn't see her at the reception desk. A double clink of a knife against a glass made me look across to the far side. It was Meila. She placed the knife across a paper napkin on the plate before saying,

'I wasn't expecting to see you until Tuesday Phill-ip, but it's a nice surprise.' We walked towards each other. I held her. She smiled and we kissed. It felt as if a capsule of love broke open inside. It was a re-affirmation of my feelings for Meila.

I now felt that the boat ride, the beach party, in fact that nothing could now affect my love for her after we kissed that time.

'Would you believe it Dan's got the day off and Bill the inspector got me to cover,' I said. We were returned to the requirements of the workplace.

'I'm short on coins. Dan said Sea View sometimes can help out.'

'How much is it you need Phill-ip?' I expect I can find coins for you, if you come over to reception. I followed Meila, who wore a short-sleeved halter-necked blue dress, with a black velvet bow at the waist level. The sculpted-out portion of dress gave an exquisite view of her sun toned back.

She looked across and smiled probably aware that I showed appreciation in my eyes.

'You just came here to change notes for coins, then?' She said after lifting the flap leading into the reception office

'No, I didn't,' I said. 'I came to see you, of course.'

'Really?'

'Really,' I said. Meila knew this perfectly well.

'I did, of course – but it's also about the beach party.'

'Oh, it's not cancelled. I was looking forward to it very much.

'No, its not cancelled it's on Thanet Island away from the beach. On the other side. Are you all right about that?'

'I'm a strong swimmer, if it sinks, I can swim.'

'I hope it doesn't come to that.'

'It sounds even more exciting now going to an island by boat than before.'

'Dan's told everyone that he's leaving with the boat at five thirty. I can be outside the Sea View by five, if you like, Meila. We'll need to walk down – the rail cars stop running at four thirty.

'But let's not meet outside the Sea View. The Blue Comet Phill-ip – it's nearer to the beach.

'That's fine by me,' I said.

I felt a sense of relief that Meila didn't consider the trip in a boat a problem. hotel was empty with all the guests out enjoying the sunshine. I asked,

'Can you manage to change forty pounds to coins?'

'How would you like this to be Phill-ip? Dan says he wants mainly one-pound coins; then fifty pence pieces and about five pounds in twenty pence pieces.'

'That's fine, Meila. Here's forty pounds,' I said, handing across two twenty-pound notes.

In the morning the foyer and breakfast area thronged with people, but now we were alone together

'I'm preparing the teas ready for Olga to serve from four to five. And you were worried about whether I could stand travelling in a boat. I practically lived in a boat when I was a child in Hong Kong. Sometimes I feel a lot safer in a boat than on land.' Meila opened a cash drawer and sorted bags of pound, fifty pence and twenty pence coins.

'That's thirty-five pounds,' she said. 'It was forty I gave you.'

'I'd not forgotten,' she said and waved a five -pound note at me.

The door from the kitchen swung open and a fair-haired girl in a waitresses' uniform came through. Meila raised her voice to call out –

'It's nearly all ready Olga,' before returning to our conversation.

'I've got to go now Phill-ip. What is your number?' Can you text me when you are near to the hotel? Here is my number to text' and she brought it up on the screen of her mobile for me to type in to mine.

'I want to make sure I'm on reception You'll visit again on Friday Phillip?'

'Yes, of course, I said, with far more confidence about the way things were going than when I first entered the hotel.

I was walking on air when I stepped out on to the veranda of Sea View. I would be seeing Pamela again. Not just when I delivered the cool boxes, but on the beach date.

I called out "great" once into the driveway, which kind of startled a couple walking their Scottie dog.

The man gave a strange, "what's gotten into him look," but the woman smiled. A number of chairs in pairs and groups across the Downs were now empty. The tickets purchased perhaps with the intention of staying for the day, but the sun was fierce in July. Many of the morning chair occupants had now gone. Mid to late afternoon others would arrive. Some, former beachgoers, where the beach trapped the sun at maximum intensity. Higher up on the Downs there was nearly always a bit of a breeze. The sail boats below looked like toy boats in a very large boating lake. Two super tankers at anchor farther out in the bay. Their cargoes gaining in value as the oil price rose. Two American cruise ships were also at anchor. The harbour at Paignton was far too shallow to accommodate these giants. Their passengers, possibly, in the nearby town bought souvenirs relating to their visit. Alongside black railings, sun flickered across glass chips within the stone path. I walked along the path, which led down to a shelter. Unless it rained or couples sought seclusion it was usually empty in the day time. The sun would be low in the sky when it finally arrived at the shelter.

I could see the bottom half of the beach path, which curved under trees and undergrowth while I walked by the empty shelter. I remembered the acute disappointment on the day following the massive rock fall to see the sign signalling the path's closure. It didn't cross my mind that a day earlier and I could have been standing underneath. Only that my source of income had dried up. That was all changed now. That event, not now seen as a disappointment, but a lucky intervention, that enabled me to take the vacancy left by Alfie.

Chapter 15

'**ARE YOU GOING TO** the beach party?' Pamela asked Olga.

'I'm going with Annie.'

'Who is Annie?' Olga lowered the tray of cups and saucers and jugs of milk on to the table as Pamela followed her across to the dining area '—and how did you get to be invited?' continued Pamela.

'It was Dan, he said that the girl Annie wanted to go, but not on her own—would I like to go with her?'

'He didn't ask you then?'

'No, but you know what he's like Pamela. He said he would've asked me, if only he'd known I wanted to go, but he wanted to take me somewhere more special and had asked a girl called Maria—pah! He thinks I believe that. It might be that young girl Annie that he has fancy for, even, who knows? I'm going to ignore him from now on, Pamela.'

'And who is this, Maria?' Asked Pamela helping Olga lay out cups and saucers on a large circular paper doily to prepare a large table set aside from the main guest tables.

'Who is she you ask? A visitor, but Dan said she is step sister to that Alfie and is here only to collect his belongings. The deck chair attendant, you know Pamela the one your boyfriend replaced.'

'Boyfriend! How do you know that he's my boyfriend Olga?'

'Pamela, you stand outside the hotel with those sparkly shoes that don't fit and your hair all special and you think no one sees you from the hotel?'

'You were spying.'

'No – you were like in full view of the hotel. Carlos came in from the kitchen and saw you talking to the deck chair attendant at the entrance. He said –

"Look, Olga there's the one who replaced Alfie—you know

Olga the one who went to the kitchen to get chicken scraps to feed his cat." I asked then to Carlos, who now looks after the cat, and it is Dan. He may not then, I think be so bad if he likes cats. What you think Pamela?'

'Yes, yes, said Pamela, but what does this Maria want here now?'

Pamela said this more speaking her thoughts aloud, than questioning Olga.

'I've told you Pamela – Dan says that this Maria is here for the deck chair attendant's belongings. How do I care what she wants? Why would I care about this new girl? Pamela I must now go to the kitchen to prepare scones and jam.

Dan said only that she is here to collect Alfie's belongings.'

'That's all Dan said?'

'Why do you ask Pamela?'

'Nothing, nothing.' Dan asked me out once, but I didn't like him. He expects every woman to be flattered by his attention and fall at his feet.

'Maybe, if you say so Pamela, but I was a very little disappointed, only a little mind, when he said he was already taking Maria to the beach party.'

'You fancy him then.'

'He's fun. He makes me laugh. The way he talks to the girls on the Downs and he tells each one she is his favourite. You hear them talk, when they come back to the hotel in the evening. They laugh about how each of them has fallen for the way he talks and jokes. How they understand that he tries to make each think she is most important girl for him, who has sat in his deck chairs.

'Perhaps he only wants one thing.'

'Then he is like most boys do you not think, who work on the beach.

Your boyfriend also?'

'I have been out with him just once. I don't know why you want to keep calling him my boyfriend, Olga. You can have

74

boyfriends like girlfriends, who you're not especially attracted to, but they can still be friends.' '–And Pamela who are you going to the beach party with– a girl friend? Or could it be Philip?'

'It happens to be Phil-ip, but I might have gone with anyone, in the way you are going with Annie. What does it matter to you, who I go with.'

'It's not matter at all Pamela, but you not say truth. You protest too much when I ask about Phillip. I'm all right to finish, if you want to go now. Are you meeting Philip later?'

'No, I'm not, and I wouldn't be telling anyone, If I was.'

'Okay, okay Pamela. We can still be friends over this. I will see you at the party and then I will know more about how it is with you and Phillip. It is no matter. Olga's smile was one of victory in the discussion.

Pamela went back to reception to pick up her handbag and some new trainers she bought in her lunch break for beach wear. Then removed the staff attendance book from the shelf above the safe. She signed the name of Pamela Evans. Evans, was the name she decided on, when her father said she would need a new name. There was a Peter Evans, who lectured in economics at Bristol Uni. The relationship never developed beyond two minds meeting in some ideological economic upland. She fell in love with the lilt of his Welsh voice. She did for a while fantasize herself into the role of the future Mrs Evans. Pamela Tomkins was, though, her name going through university.

Shortly after leaving Sea View, she placed the key in the door of her mother's flat.

'What's the matter Pamela?' asked her mother when she thought the flat door slammed rather too loudly on Pamela's return.

'Nothing, it's just been a boring afternoon at the hotel.' 'Look at these Pamela,' said Rita as Pamela entered the sitting room.

Her mother produced several photos of shops up for let in the town centre.

'They're all in ideal position.'

'Why do you think I'd be interested?'

'You might show interest Pamela. I don't know what you think you'll do when summer season is ended at Sea View.'

'I'll find something. That's miles away.' Pamela caught her face in the mirror over the fireplace and noticed freckles were visible again around her nose, while she pondered about what Olga said about Philip being her boyfriend. It was her business and nothing to do with the likes of Olga.

'Olga's going from the hotel to the party on Friday.' 'That's good I've met Olga. She is a polite girl, very sensible.'

'When and how did you meet her mother?' Pamela sat in the armchair by the fire and picked up the photos her mother had placed on the coffee table.

'I went for a coffee on the veranda with Mr Timmins the estate agent and it was Olga, who served us—this morning, very sweet girl. You wouldn't have seen us from where you were at the reception. I also spoke with Mr Langridge. A very pleasant man.'

'Yes, he's the hotel manager – I can't believe you breezed into the hotel Mother?'

'Why not?' It helps to know who is there. To be sure there is no one suspicious.'

'You might've been seen as suspicious. What if someone saw the likeness?'

'They didn't. You're paler skinned, very slim – A little too slim, I think.

There isn't much of a resemblance.'

'Thank goodness for that.' Rita smiled, exaggeratedly at Pamela in reply.

'Do you have a half day on Friday Pamela? she asked. 'Yes, I'm planning to go to the shops.'

'I'll come with you. I have appointments to view the properties —you can help me choose. I like them all from the out-side. They're in a good position for the passengers from the ships. Your father doesn't want to use the beach as a delivery point much longer. He says there are too many risks. Too many people involved. You can help me make a choice.'

'If I must Mother – but not all afternoon. I'll give you an hour, that's all.'

'Perhaps I can be of help with a new dress?'

'There's no need to bribe me – I'm volunteering—I don't want a dress, but then perhaps you could help to buy a beach towel and sun glasses.

There isn't likely to be much sun in the evening Pamela and won't the hotel have a spare towel?'

'Yes, but I need one that is green to match my bikini and sun glasses are more a fashion statement. It's not just about the sun – and aren't you the fashion expert Mother?'

Chapter 16

IT'S COME THROUGH JULIE – the payment.' Julie snapped the shutter down at the same time as Bill closed the door into the ticket office.

'We can view the flat tomorrow according to the estate agent.'

'Which one is it asked Julie?' She clicked the kettle on. Bill took his cap off and with a practiced throw flung it on to a hook before sitting in the wicker chair.

'It's the one overlooking the quayside with the balcony. Above the café. I said I preferred that one to the others we looked over.' Julie sat on the ticket desk and pointed to a framed photo she'd positioned on the table next to the kiosk.

'Isn't he cute. The photographer from the Evening Express was on the promenade taking pictures of contestants for their beautiful baby competition. I told him Buggles was my baby and he took a photo of us together.' In the photo Julie was standing on the promenade with her back to the beach in a red bikini. Her right arm was raised and the photo showed Buggles jumping to take half a biscuit from her hand. He'd caught the moment when the dog's feet were off the ground and his mouth partly open to take hold of the biscuit.

'My hair was blowing everywhere, but he caught a good photo of Buggles, don't you think Billy?'

'The dog's looking okay, but for me it's you in that red bikini.

You'd look smashing on a magazine cover, never mind the dog. I bet the photographer was thinking much the same.' Bill picked the photo up to bring it into better light before returning it to the desk.

'Do I detect a little jealousy? I don't belong to you. We're still both married, you know,' Julie said

'I do know that,' said Bill.

78

'But that's the reason we're getting the flat. We can live together and after two years get married.'

'The flat will be in joint names?'

'Yes.' Julie crossed her arms and stood up. With her fingers, she hitched the bottom of her blouse away from the skirt, accompanying this with a sideway smile toward Bill. An invitation perhaps. Bill walked across and kissed her neck. Julie's hair was clustered in a coiffured display on top leaving an expanse of neck available to be kissed. Julie answered with a kiss on his cheek, by which time Bill was unbuttoning the blouse. Their relationship more assured than at the start of the summer season. There was now a more leisurely approach to love making. The real prospect of a flat and a future together away from the work environment meant she felt more able to build a life that might still require reactivating memories of Carl, but not have to contend with the dalliances of Terry with each new female employee who was enrolled for shadowing.

'He's taking out that Asian receptionist at the Sea View,' she said to Bill.

'Who is?'

'The new deck chair attendant. He's shown me pencil sketches of her. They're good. I wish I could sketch like that and he did them from memory – after work – in his flat. He must be really taken with her. He's nearly filled a sketch book with them.

'What without any clothes on.'

'No of course not!' They're sketches of her working behind the reception desk at Sea View. They're about the same age. Doesn't it occur to you Bill that they might just like each other's company and like a bit of intelligent conversation.

'Not in that case. The other attendants were chasing her before that Phil came on the scene – and it wasn't just because she has a degree in higher education.

Chapter 17

I WAS BACK ON the Downs and the problem that Meila might not want to go to Thanet Island by motor boat was resolved. It was even better she'd texted her number into my mobile. We could keep in touch about what was happening.

Psychological studies suggest that the like and dislike mechanism, which is within each of us requires about two minutes to decide on whether we like or dislike a person on first meeting. So much, I thought, for all the hype about getting to know someone through shared interests. That first hurdle is a crucial one of whether you like each other. I'm certain I jumped that one in under the designated two minutes. That first glimpse of Meila at reception, or Pamela, as I knew her then was more like a spear entering heart and cortex, but with a delightful and paralyzing intensity. Initial intuitive reaction plays a key part. Attraction, though is something else. So instantaneous and breath-taking that it can leave you stunned. In the sense that you want to express your feelings for the person in words, but also aware that there isn't a total certainty that she shares the same depth of feeling. The mind can play tricks with you. The kiss in the veranda of the Blue Comet was something else. That it said to me we were more than just a couple who were on a first date. That level of intimacy, which transcends the moment. But cruelly minutes before we met again at Sea View there was, I doubting that it ever happened.

Those doubts vanished the moment she walked towards me in the hotel, and stopped so close that she intended that we should kiss. I was in there, but in the way of a greeting, no more. It was four o'clock. Half an hour since I left Sea View on that crucial Sunday. I did a sweep across the Downs, including the balcony, which caught a few deck chair customers, who might have believed they were safe from a visit.

Unusually exhilarated for the time of day I decided to visit Mrs Brown at the Red and White Rose café. Not to exchange coins for notes, but for a chat. I didn't reckon on a visit by the area beach inspector late in the day. A lowered sun caused a golden reflection across the bay. The red and white cafe awning, glistened in the bright light, and shadowed the pavement on the other side of the Downs Road. It was then that I spotted Dan walking along the front – in jeans, tee shirt and flip flops. I nearly mistook him for another holiday maker.

'What you doing this evening?' He shouted from the other side of the road.

'Nothing special – can't you keep away on your day off?'

'I've got to order sausages from the butcher for the party and this is my shortest route into town. Is that a problem?' I crossed the road.

'No just remarking, that's all,' I continued,

'Cliff Side tonight, Phil?'

'Might as well—are you taking Maria?'

'You know Maria? How d'you know Maria?' It was getting like the Song from The Sound of Music

'She was sat on the balcony earlier, saying where's Dan? That's how I know.'

'You know who she is then?'

'Yes, Alfie's step-sister.' A car went by halting our conversation.

'She wanted to know where Alfie worked and I said he did this job, but on the beach. Then she asked if I knew where they found Alfie. That led me to inviting Maria to the beach party and I said I'd show her the exact spot where he was found.

We're not meeting again until after work on Friday. Anything else Mr Inquisitor?' I can guess where you're going,' said Dan— 'Mrs Brown's café. But not to get hold of coins because you've been to the Sea View—am I right? Does she still want to go to the beach party?'

'Yes, but no thanks to you telling me the parties on Thanet

Island after I'd made out it was on Babbacombe beach,' I replied. I could've done without meeting Dan. to change the subject I said,

'Does Reggie, put in a Sunday afternoon appearance?'

'Never known him drive around late afternoon, save on Friday and that's to take wages to the beach. You're quite safe Phil. See you about eight-ish, then at Cliff Side.'

Dan continued walking along the Downs towards the butcher. I went up the steps into the café. The sunny afternoon meant there was only Ambrose sat half way back, with time on his hands – with every intention of making his coffee last as long as a three -course meal. I didn't want to get involved. He caught me the first time when I went in to exchange notes for coins. Fortunately, this time, his head was stuck in the Sporting Life. I sat on a stool by the counter well clear of the window. He played piano or electric keyboard.

Mainly to fund his horse racing it appeared. The intention that his winnings could fund a minimalist work lifestyle, I imagined. He complained to me when I met him on the Downs how the guests at the hotels lacked taste.

'All they want is brash music from shows,' he said dismissively, as if that was an insult to his musicianship. 'They never want Strauss or Chopin.' He once played the Blue Danube in the foyer of Sea View during afternoon teas. I felt that, the composer, if alive might have passed on picking Ambrose as his pianist. He did say he played for a big band in his youth. I made the mistake of sitting opposite him on my first visit

'There're perks from playing at hotels,' he said. 'Vera,' – one of the guests, sold me this for ten pounds. He then raised his left arm pulled back the sleeve and displayed a Rolex watch.

Ambrose was one of several beach scene players, I felt, who sought to exploit the vulnerable and lonely in the summer. In winter, he told me, he dressed in a suit and bow tie and made out he was an antiques expert. He undervalued pieces of furniture on house visits. Then made a tidy profit at the local auction. Otherwise known as a knocker, who is as disingenuous about giving a fair price as a hooker is about offering love.

From the stool I could see the row of tin trays. Customers paid a deposit to ensure the trays return from the downs. Set out with doily, cups and saucers, milk jugs and sugar bowls. Small and large stainless-steel teapots, lids up, ready for action ranged around the water boiler. The glass display cabinet featured scones, pots of jam and apple pie cut in squares from the Sea View, plus a selection of sandwiches in cellophane wrap. Dan was on first names, and would talk about Stella rather than Mrs Brown. She walked out from the back with a box of PG Tips teabags, which she placed next to the teapots. White haired with a green overall dress, blue apron, and a white circular hat.

'No coins required today then?' 'Well, no,' I said.

'That's all right. Dan cleared me out when he visited on Tuesday and it's mainly the time of week, I need coins myself.

'What can I get you?'

'A cool drink. A Coke would be fine Mrs Brown.

Chapter 18

'IT'S ALL RIGHT THERE'S a bus—your father says there is a bus.' Pamela and her mother were stood on the main road into town at a bus stop.

'In London there is not just the one option. I would call a taxi,' said Rita.

'Well, you could've done that today,' said Pamela, holding the umbrella near to keep the rain from her hair. Rita wore a scarf unperturbed by the rain. The complaining ended when the top of the double decker bus could be seen at the brow of the hill. Pamela was quick to put her hand out knowing her mother would expect the bus to stop for her without any instructions.

The driver smiled at Pamela as she boarded, having stopped directly where she was standing, although away from the actual stop. She smiled back after shaking the umbrella before folding it. Her mother paid the fare.

'Two for the town centre driver please.' The glass partition around the driver vibrated noisily with the engine turning over at low speed. Pamela walked halfway back and sat next to the window in front of two rather glum looking holiday-makers.

'I've got to go to the estate agents first. He'll be coming with us,' said her mother as she grabbed the chrome support by the seat before sitting down.

'He's not going to be with us all afternoon, is he?' 'No, but he has to let us in.'

'Like we'll run off with the keys,' said Pamela.

'He has a job to do. Nice well-spoken young man, about your age, very suitable husband material.' Pamela poked her tongue out and made as if to be sick.

'Don't do that in public ever again Pamela when you're with me.'

'That I could ever fall for an estate agent Mother.' Rita turned toward the far window and said,

'That's something I would like. An estate agent for a son in law could be very useful.' The bus doors shut, but they only moved a short distance before they flapped open again. Pamela recognized the man boarding. It was the occasional pianist who played at the Sea View.

'A single to the town centre,' he said – thanks for stopping.'

The estate agents were on a hill leading away from the town centre past where the bus stopped. A three-minute walk and the A board outside was visible plus the green and yellow sign suspended above that declared Atkins & Simpson, estate Agents. A wire rack ran alongside the outer window holding paper blurb about houses they had to sell. The bell above the door rang when opened. The premises were once a real shop and retained this quaint reminder of those days when the shopkeeper might have been out the back and needing to know that a customer was in the shop.

'Mrs Tompkins so nice to see you again. A grey suited brown wavy-haired man in his mid-twenties with a blue hand-kerchief in his top packet with matching tie stood up from a desk to the left of the door.

'You've come to look at suitable premises for a boutique. They're all in walking distance you'll be pleased to know Mrs Tomkins and hello,' he turned to speak to Pamela, who was completing the colouring – in of her early picture of an estate agent more than adequately.

'This is Pamela my daughter. She is very interested to see the boutiques as I am Mr Timmins'

'How nice to meet you, Pamela.' He could have held out his hand, but must have detected a certain coldness on Pamela's part.

'That's great then.' He kept a smile in place while calling out. 'Angelica we'll be needing the boutique keys,' to a young woman, spinning a display unit around in the opposite window, with a stack nearby of notices for new listings. She nodded and placed the photos on the green felted window ledge beneath the stands and walked across to a floor safe at the back – requisitioned for storage of house and shop keys.

'Do have a seat both of you. Is there anything you'd like to ask before we visit? Can I offer you a coffee?'

'Afterwards maybe. How much free rent are the landlord or landlords, prepared to offer?' Said Rita before sitting in one of the two chairs in front of his desk. Rita, liked to be direct about what really mattered and couldn't do with over much frivolous chat, when business was on the agenda.

'That's something I could look into for you Mrs Tomkins.'

Pamela looked at her mother askance for her forthright approach.

'They're very desirable premises for a retailer.'

'Not that desirable – they have been unoccupied for over six months.' Rita did her homework before they left London. Pamela wanted to disappear into the floor, particularly after Mr Timmins kept flitting his eyes across to look at her crossed legs from his raised chair. She begun to wish she'd worn jeans or a trouser suit instead of a skirt and even gone without placing cream over her freckles. Was this worth going through just because her mother would pay for a new towel and sun glasses. The disappointing answer was probably yes, given the fact that pay day was two weeks away.

Angelica crossed over to the farthest wall from the safe and appeared to study a sales graph. This was a joint exercise, because apart from seeking to show interest in the graph in sight of Mr Timmins it also allowed her silhouette to pass before him and hopefully draw more attention to the fact that she was in high heels and wearing the mini skirt that led to her being sent home early by the head teacher when in the sixth form two years previously. She held the circular tray, like a waitress. The tray depicted a country cottage in a flowered garden, with three bunches of keys evenly spaced at the edge.

He didn't look at her once, as she approached, but managed a "thank you Angelica" after the tray contacted the desk noisily enough to interrupt their conversation.

'Will you be wanting me to assist at the viewing Nige?' She smiled appealingly at her boss.

'No, you can continue replacing the window display this time.'

Pamela was given a frosty look, but felt like saying out loud— 'He's all yours Angelica.'

Chapter 19

'WE'RE READY WHEN YOU are,' Rita said to the estate agent, who pulled open a drawer and produced a blue file marked in black Sharpie – MRS RITA TOMPKINS along the top flap. He stood up and called across to Angelica – 'Won't be long Ange.' The door bell's abrupt ring prevented further conversation until the three of them were on the street outside.

'Are you settling in Mrs Tomkins? – It must seem very quiet compared to city life,' he said after he followed the two women through the shop door.

'Quiet is good for me,' she said.

'All three shops, are near to us, as you know. Down the road, round the corner and the first street on the right. The first one was once a fish mongers.' Pamela screwed her nose up at the remark.

'I'm in no great hurry,' said Rita when the pace quickened. She was five foot nothing. His look back, more a smile for Pamela than in reassurance that he would slow his walk – but he did. The street was no entry, and cars couldn't park anywhere in the high street. Paignton's multi-story car park, was inadequate during the summer months and motorists were encouraged to park and ride. The town centre's road was tarmacked but the side street cobbled with rows of small shops on both sides. It was the fourth one down next to a hairdresser.

'Yes, I like this position next to a hairdresser,' Rita said. There were six women seated and being attended to and several being served coffee in a cordoned off area with cosy chairs and a photo gallery of styled models on the back wall. The peeling blue paint and sun-bleached brown paper covered the windows of the first shop, but were less problematical when the position was considered. Nigel quick to make the point that it was well positioned for possible clientele, regardless of the run -down state.

'Seven, seven,' he said as he looked at the three possible choices of door keys before he located a brass tag with seven on it and placed the other two back in his pocket. He opened the lower and top lock with a long key and then while turning the Yale key pushed the door with his knee at the same time. 'There's no electric, but I've armed myself with a torch,' he said, which he produced from inside his jacket pocket, switched on and gave to Pamela.

'I'll pull the paper back to let some light in.' There was a rubbery smell which mingled with dust thrown up by the door opening. When they walked in the sun's rays caught the newly disturbed dust as Nigel lifted two strips of brown paper behind the window.

'It's twelve hundred square feet.' You mentioned a floor space of one thousand Mrs Tomkins.'

'Did I,' said Rita, with her upper lip curled upwards in disapproval at what she saw and smelt. The smell was from the underlay which remained after the carpet was removed. A brown sponge expanse broken by white patches of flooring. The edges of the underlay jagged and shrunken. Outer edges turned black from long time exposure to air and light – what light there was.

'Let me have the torch a moment?' Rita said to Pamela. Nigel was left standing holding the paper away from the shop window. Rita shown the torch on to the ceiling. There were cracked asbestos tiles. Testimony to the age of the shop and its time out of use.

'Ten thousand at the very least to replace those.

– 'No, I'm looking for more ready to go than this.'

'It's in good condition otherwise,' said Pamela. Rita flashed the torch across the side walls and back then handed the torch back to Nigel, who dropped the brown window paper. It was already crinkled by previous attempts to let in light. Light leaked through at the top of the shop windows, but it was an oasis of calm inside from the bustle outside. The paper slipped back down across the window, and left them in near darkness before he held open the door for them to leave.

'The next one is in better condition, but this one is in a good position you'll agree.'

'Yes, but not for me,' said Rita. Any free rent would be lost getting it ready for trading.'

'Not to worry, the next one is in really good shape, 'said Nigel kneeling to put the key in the bottom door lock. It is one street up – the other side of Cross Street, and is at the end of the quayside. Now part of this vibrant shopping venue.' Rita turned to Pamela, believing she was out of earshot and said 'Not that vibrant by the look of things,' pointing to a boarded up former bakers opposite to where they were standing.

'I completely understand what you are saying Mrs Tompkins, but I think the next one you will like. It's no distance.' They started walking.

'Will it be a family business?' he asked. 'Mother and daughter perhaps?'

'It is what I do,' said Rita. 'It is a private business,' bringing further questioning to an end. Not wanting to answer questions, that she considered intrusive.

Chapter 20

I BALANCED THE TICKET collection money in the gardeners shed and walked into the theatre foyer to hand over the day's takings. That was the arrangement. Amie, the theatre cashier pulled the shutter down and checked the amount £140-25: before signing in the cashier's box at the side. I phoned Aunt Sue in Harpenden, not every week, but quite often – whenever I decided I could do with some of her down to earth talk. She was my father's sister and gave access to family on a more indirect basis. To my knowledge the trauma of my leaving the bank still un-subsided.

'Lost opportunity, and if only I'd had such opportunity, when I was your age.' – I remembered these words from my father as though they were spoken yesterday. He was the manager of a small supermarket and regularly complained about working out of hours.

'Banks have regular hours and there's cheap loan money. You will regret it later I can tell you.'

I returned to the gardener's shed to lock away the ticket machine, leather money pouch and takings book in the cupboard and put the key back under the brick on the floor.

My portfolio range of evening meals consisted of boil in the bag kipper, a selection of things on toast. Baked beans, scrambled egg, and sardines on toast were all possible choices where time allowed for preparation. Otherwise, a ready meal. I was not a great fan of pasties and pies, but some variety of sandwich could be concocted, when the bread was newly purchased and not a potential candidate for Alexander Fleming to prove his discovery.

I'd bought a small sliced loaf two days ago and decided on corn beef sandwiches.

Dan's mention of visiting the butcher prompting me to consider a meat option which required minimal preparation.

The butcher was four streets up from Acacia Avenue, which took me past Sea View. This made me wonder where Meila was now. The knowledge that I would be seeing her tomorrow lifted my spirits. Tonight, it was ham sandwiches and a peach yoghurt, from the small fridge.

I stopped off at the butchers. On opening the door, I was greeted by 'You're not wanting sausages, are you?' the butcher broke off from cutting up lamb chops with his cleaver.

'That Dan's cleaned us out. There all in the fridge for Saturday.'

'No just a few slices of ham,' I said. 'That's no problem.' Three, slices – alright?'

'Yep, that's okay,' I said, and he picked the ham up with tongs, weighed it, and placed it into a polythene bag.

'There you are—just one pound fifty.' I took the ham and handed over a two-pound coin and walked back to the flat. It was on the first-floor landing of a Victorian house. Apart from an elaborate Victorian style porch entrance the inside was completely modernized.

A once very large hall way had been converted into a ground floor flat as had the two large adjoining rooms. A quite narrow corridor ran along the centre. The original stairway replaced with a metal one with hand rails on each side which led to my first floor flat.

Both floors shared their own bathroom and separate toilet. The original kitchen on the ground floor was a communal one. It was built with students in mind. Babbacombe College was nearby.

I showered, shaved, and changed into jeans and tee shirt. Went down stairs and along a corridor, which led to the kitchen. A kitchen shared on trust.

This did seem to work with each flat allocated separate wall cupboards for food and utensils.

I was inserting the ham between the slices of buttered bread when Debbie from the upstairs flat opposite mine arrived by the kitchen door.

'Phil so glad you're in,' she said. Dark hair normally pony-tailed or scrunched up in some fashion, for work; now released, to spread across her shoulders. A quilted dressing gown sort of acted as a passion killer to the luxuriant spread of hair. Liz her flat mate, some would say was more attractive, in a model type figure kind of way.

I met Debbie and Liz, in the communal lounge, on arrival. They were working for the summer as English teachers to the droves of Swedish and French students that were billeted in Babbacombe for the summer months. The Swedish parents perhaps escaped to chalets in the fjords or maybe with the French parents, their chateaus in the country.

'Liz said, that she thought you might have some plain flour. It's not important if you haven't. Perhaps a long shot,' and gave a smile that said she wouldn't be disappointed with my not having plain flour, but I was pleased with my reply.

'I do have a box of plain flour, as a matter of fact.' She produced a cup from behind her back.

'Just half a cup,' she said, looking innocently at me.

'Liz was right after all – I said you probably wouldn't have any flour.'

'Is half a cup enough?'

'It's only to dust fish fillets before putting them in the pan—that's all.'

'I'll get it for you. She held the cup by the handle and placed it in my open hand. I walked back towards the kitchen and left the door wide open. With a hand on the door frame Debbie stepped forward. This movement allowed a glimpse of leg before the dressing gown regained its closed position.

'You're looking cool I normally only see you in your beach uniform.' With a remark like that and a week ago, before I'd met Meila, I would have replied with—

'Do you fancy going to the Cliff Side for a drink?' The belief in place that this was on the cards, if not that night, then another night.

Chapter 21

I GRABBED THE VARNISHED railing, which led up to the Cliff Side hotel entrance, on the Thursday before the beach party. The building perched on a granite outcrop. It was an unusual geological formation amongst the red sandstone which occupied adjoining cliffs around this coastline, but a solid foundation for the beach hotel – also open to non-residents.

I knew that Dan was taking Maria to the barbecue and considered he might already have taken her out. But realized that for Maria, it was not just a holiday visit. More, like a memorial visit to get a sense of the place in which her step brother met his death, than that of a holiday. It was evident that in despite of Bill's astonishment that Alfie wasn't that interested in money, he did enjoy his work. Dan said afterwards that beach goers from a previous year who had known Alfie, remarked on how welcoming he was when they met up again for the new season and that he so enjoyed beach work. It upset everyone I met, except perhaps Bill, to learn of his passing away. It was generally accepted that it wasn't such a bad away to die, while in an occupation you enjoyed. Now, a fortnight after he was buried Maria had travelled from Gallway Bay to collect his few belongings and find out more.

I already knew Dan was there, because a black mountain bike was padlocked to the railings, which ran down to the beach. His bike might still be there the following morning. This didn't look a likely prospect when I entered and saw Dan stood alone by the bar. He must have just arrived before me, and trying to catch the bar man's eye to get a Fosters. Dan remained loyal to whichever holiday maker he took out, at least until their stay was over and I'm pretty sure he paid his way. Unlike Ambrose, who made no qualms about sponging off visitors. Dan turned away from the bar as I approached.

'Phil what are you having to drink. Some of the golden nectar?' Meaning Fosters.

'No, I'll stick to a half of Butcombe bitter Dan.'

Plastic lobsters dangled from a fish net above the fireplace. This upset a sense of authenticity. Netting, supported by a pair of deep-sculpted long bladed oars tipped together over the fire place, one red one blue. Attached floats, did emit sea salt drenched stench, acquired by previously sea immersed cork. Ships, in bottles decorated a mantle shelf. More, in the fireplace. Driftwood-shaped into sharks with painted white teeth and black fins. Weathered beach wood was nearly effective as a gull on the wall with orange beak and streaky grey white paint plumage. Plastic lobsters, just ruined it for me. I was not attending to Dan, who wanted to attract the bar man's attention.

'Where are you, Phil? – As if I didn't know, you could've asked her out tonight.'

'Who?

Who? Who you ask? Look mate I've reliable info that you were with that foxy minx from Sea View – at the Blue Comet. Why didn't you get her to come along? Now you're stuck with your old mate Dan.'

'Perhaps, because I knew I was meeting up with you?'

'Can't face competition then?'

'It's only a holiday romance when you take a girl out. You've told me that yourself.' Not wanting to let on how smitten I was with Pamela, who anyway was now Meila to me and always would be. I tried to sound nonchalant and indifferent to the idea that Meila might mean anything more to me, than, a holiday romance I remember, at the time.

'Yes sir? The pony-tailed barman flung a white cloth he held, across his shoulder, and eyeballed Dan in a way that suggested the added "sir" was affected.

'Can I take your order?' He was wearing a waiter's coat, which indicated that he doubled up with the role of bar man.

I turned away to look across the bar while Dan was placing the drinks order. On the stairway on a landing area just above the bar I caught sight of a dark-haired girl, who leant across and looked toward the other side of the bar. Perhaps for someone she knew? A red tunic blouse, and black jeans against a greenish décor of the stairway. She turned and I realized it was Maria. She walked over to the banister rail nearest to us.

'I see your latest girlfriend's here,' I said to Dan, who was waiting for the drinks to arrive.

'How do you mean?' I pointed to the stairway. Maria, hadn't noticed us. The tables and chairs around the stairs beneath were occupied and she appeared to be deciding whether to venture down.

'Heck,' said Dan, she must be staying here. Never told me.'

Dan walked away just as the barman placed the drinks in front of him.

'I'll pay,' I said, and produced a ten-pound note and felt a frisson of relief when I saw Maria's face change from one of aloneness to a smile, when she spotted Dan's familiar face. Dark bushy hair and eyebrows, together with an easy charm was a winning formula with the opposite sex it seemed.

He reached out and took her hand as Maria arrived on the final stairs. It would perhaps, have been better inviting Pamela, but then not! I could've asked her out after I met Dan on the Downs, but it was very early in the relationship and I didn't want to rush in and spoil how things were between us. Neither of us, that's Dan and me knew Maria was staying at the Cliff Side. She must have booked in recently, otherwise Dan would have met her there before when not in his role as deck chair attendant.

They manoeuvred their way back, through tables where customers were either eating or waiting for a meal.

'I never knew you were staying here,' said Dan as they reached me by the bar.

'You've met Phil?' She smiled and said — 'Hi-yah Phil–

96

I'm only here for one more night. I'm moving in with Sal tomorrow to share. Is this your local?'

'It is for Dan,' I said. Dan offered to get Maria a drink.

'Thanks Dan I'll have a Coke please. —I've just got Alfie's things back from the police. I'll need work to stay here any longer. A will's been found. It's gone to probate. I don't even know if he's left me anything. He may have left what he had to a cat's home. I don't really care. I would rather Alfie was still here, of course.' The bar area was free and I listened to Maria as Dan bought her a Coke.

'It must have been a shock to hear about it the way you did,' I said.

'He was careful with money, but he was taken up with the job. He said it reminded him of his days on the trawlers working by the sea and how now the salt air helped with his breathing.

'Bill, the inspector told me that a shoe box was jammed with bundles of notes when he visited your step brother's flat. They were the equivalent to eighteen months wages,' I said. 'It seems that he must've lived on his fireman's pension.' I wanted to make sure Maria knew about this, in case this money somehow went missing.

'I honestly really do not care about how much he left. He was just a lovely sort of person,' said Maria, with a faraway look in her eyes. He wrote and said how much he liked his job. Judging by the look on Dan's face he was like the Beach Inspector troubled relating to the idea that someone might work, because they enjoyed the company, the outdoor life, and the fresh sea air, rather from a need to purely earn cash.

A couple were leaving a table in an alcove opposite. I suggested we could sit there.

Dan had paid for the coke with lemon and ice, requested by Maria when the girl Sal, walked out from the back – now attired in a blue coat with the words Cliff Side Hotel embroidered, on the front pocket.

'Sal,' called out Maria in recognition, who then came over to where the three of us were sitting. The best part of fifteen minutes passed by while the two of them talked. Dan meanwhile, was all hyped up about the beach barbecue.

'I've got the charcoal, matches, a bottle of meths to help it on its way, but no grill.'

'A man in love with Ozz like you Dan—wouldn't imagine getting a barbie together would be a problem.'

'They have all the kit in their gardens or stored in a garage. It is just part of household equipment. They don't have to improvise, Phil,' he said.

'There'll be pebbles and rocks on the beach. You just need a metal grid to go on top. My port of call is a scrap car merchant for something like that.

Probably got cooking tongs and such like at the beach café. You just need to build a wall of rocks and place the grid on top. Set it alight, a good two hours before you need it.'

'Okay, sounds good. That's where you can help Phil. We can go out in the boat in the afternoon. Set it up and come back.'

'I have to be back by four,' I said.

'We'll manage that, easy,' said Dan, nearly downing his Fosters in one go. Dan was not inquisitive, but I did not want to explain that I was to meet up with Pamela at five.

Maria, excited, after her chat with Sal tipped some Coke on to the table, whilst putting the glass down.

'I've got a job here starting tomorrow. I can pay for the flat share and stay while everything is being sorted out. She sat next to Dan, in the alcove window. The boys' night out now definitely on hold.

'Alfie left a will. ' it's gone to probate, but I may not stay much longer. I haven't decided.

'Yes, you said, earlier. I take it you figure in the will?' Asked Dan.'

'Would that make me more attractive, then, if I do?'

I felt Dan had met his match with Maria at an early stage in their meeting.

'Alfie was seventeen years older and from my step mothers first marriage. He was twenty-eight when I arrived on the scene. I was adopted. He became more like a father than elder brother and we've kept in touch since he moved to England from Gallway. My step parents are very elderly. They moved to Australia, after I left Uni. Alfie never married. I was planning to come and see him this Summer, but not expecting to in this way.' It went quiet for a while both Dan and I not knowing what to say.

Sal was collecting glasses on a tray and arrived at our table, which broke the silence.

'You're coming to the party Sal,' aren't you,' said Dan.

'I've got no one to go with.'

'Yes, you have, you can join me and Dan,' said Maria.

Maria was not the compliant kind of girl Dan normally went for—though it can be that the quiet ones, who are the more controlling – once you are written into a future contract. Outspokenness in the public domain could perhaps mask a more subdued little woman demeanor than when alone with a partner. In the early stages, it's easy to believe you've hitched up with a princess, with all that sweetness and charm front of house. The other side held in abeyance before the catch is netted, so to speak. But then the girl might say she has to kiss lots of princes before she meets her very own frog, and to be sure he will not hop away.

Chapter 22

I LOOKED AT MY watch when I spoke, that way you do to emphasis a sense of urgency when in company. It is a fabrication to look as if you have something very important to deal with and it's slipped, your mind.

'I promised to call someone. Is that the time?' I turned seeking clarity from the ship's clock in the centre of the wheel behind the bar.

'I'll be back,' I said. Now, the proverbial gooseberry I decided that I might as well call Aunt Sue. It was an escape route. There was a lobby to the side of the bar next to a conservatory, which was curtained off for the night. Nine-fifteen, later than I might normally have called – but not that late! I remembered the number – 01582 226674. The only phone number that stuck in my mind at the time. A sign on the door said push, which I did. I sat down at a table and chairs that was tucked into the corner, while the door finished closing behind me. I scrolled to find the number on my phone and waited for the dial tone.

'Sue Stapleton speaking.' 'Hello Aunt Sue.'

'Phillip – and where are you or is it that no one's supposed to know?'

This was asked as if I was on some clandestine voyage 'I'm on the south coast at Babbacombe.'

'Babbacombe – right, doing what? Not working at a bank—I take it?'

'Spot on. I'm selling deck chair tickets.'

'You sound happy by the tone of your voice.'

'I'm okay. I've met someone at the Sea View. She's a receptionist.'

'I remember the Sea View. It faces on to the Downs. Is she some local girl working there?'

'No, she's originally from Hong Kong, father British and

100

mother Chinese, but she went to school here before going to Bristol University.'

'Very attractive and perhaps fairly petite?'

'Well yes, but— how?'

'That girl Ann, from art college fitted that description — that's all. I'm pleased for you Phil.' I changed the subject,

'How are things at home?'

'You mean at your home. Desperate. Very desperate. Your father can't believe that you don't want to have a career in banking. I told him he's living in the past, expecting kids to want to stick to one career. But your father is the eldest and expects everyone to do as he says. I should know. I only escaped when I married your Uncle Steve.' This gave reassurance that what I'd done wasn't so abnormal as my immediate family made out. In part, the reason for calling Aunt Sue.

'What's that?' Aunt Sue broke off to listen to Uncle Steve in the background. She continued,

'Babbacombes got quite a reputation for gangs and drug running so your uncle tells me.' It wasn't going to be one of those man to aunt conversations I'd hoped for now I knew there was the CCTV camera effect of Uncle Steve.

'I've not seen any. It's a sleepy sort of place, filled with holidaymakers and people like me looking after them, making the most of the fresh air and sunshine.'

'That's right Phillip sleepy is the word I'd use. They do like to "big things up," in news bulletins, especially when it's away London's hub. Your uncle Steve's a sucker for anything a good-looking woman news reader tells him on the flat screen.'

'What's that you said Susan?' Uncle Steve homing in again at the mention of his name.

'Nothing dear, just telling Phillip how you're looking forward to the start of the football season.' I'd never considered that Uncle Steve was hard of hearing, but judging by the way Sue was able to make up a story out of what had been said, suggested this could be so.

101

'Where are you now Phillip.'

'I'm in the lobby at the side of the Cliff Side bar. Dan, who works with me on the deck chairs has met with a girlfriend.'

'And you decided to phone your Aunt Susan. Where's your receptionist girlfriend?'

'I've only been out with her once.'

'The Cliff Side's quite upmarket from what I can remember, you should've invited her.' Aunt Sue continued talking about her recollections of the Cliff Side, while the door opened from the bar and a couple in jeans and tee shirts tumbled into the lobby. The girl allowed herself to be held against the opposite wall. They were oblivious to my sitting at the table. The boyfriend then took hold of the back of her head like you might a large apple in preparation for a bite. She put an arm around him. Upturned, smiling face confirmed that the pinning against the wall met with approval. Passionate kissing resulted. They were against the opposite wall. The girl even if she saw me didn't seem to be bothered. Perhaps, I had achieved invisibility, but this may have been a repeat performance for the two of them and they were too wrapped up in one another to notice—not just physically!

This was probably the case, because the boy extricated himself from the girl's advanced embrace and opened the curtains and door leading out to the conservatory. They both went through and the curtains closed. My role of unplanned voyeur ended. I returned to Aunt Sue's elaboration on her memories of the Cliff Side.

'Are you listening Phillip?' I had missed an appropriate, "yes" or "no."

'Cliff Side was considered very acceptable when I holidayed there. You talked earlier about sketching Phil?'

'Yes, that was going all right until the cliff path got covered with a rock fall. They were advertising for a deck chair attendant on the beach and I went for it.'

'That's okay then, I can tell your father you've got a job and

102

not just sketching. You know how he does not see painting, writing, or acting as meaningful work.'

'I do,' I said.

'You're father resented accompanying our father – your grand-dad— on the piano when he sang and told jokes on stage. He now has a particular aversion to the performing arts and as for painters he says they sleep penniless in a garret and only paint satisfactorily when they are starving.'

'Yes, I've heard all that Aunt Sue.'

'I'm taking Meila to a beach barbecue this Saturday.'

'That's a nice name.'

'She adopted the name Pamela after the family came to England, but she prefers her birth name and likes friends to call her Meila.'

'This Meila must like you a lot then. I hope you both enjoy the barbecue, don't get carried away – make sure you use protection, if the situation arises.'

'Aunt Sue! When did you become a family advisory counsellor?'

'I'm just warning you—if a woman decides she wants a man to be the father of her children she can let it happen and not take precautions.'

There were half-stifled cries from the conservatory, which worked in unison with a regular tap of an uneven table leg, disturbed by rhythmic pressure from presumably the girl being laid across the table. I hoped that he was taking the precautions that Aunt Sue was suggesting. It sounded as if it was a bit too late for the man now, if they were not.

'I'm just offering a little advice about how women are not always what they seem to a man.'

'I just don't think it applies in this situation, aunt Sue.' The interruption by Dan was not unwelcome in that aunt Sue was in lecture mood and I only wanted chat. He pushed open the door and stood in front of the table jigging about on the floor. Seeing that I was on my mobile – he mouthed the words

"Blue Comet" a couple of times – like some lunatic who had lost power of speech.

'I'd best be going aunt – it's been nice talking to you. All the best to Uncle Steve. I hope I didn't ring too late.'

'Call anytime you like Phillip, except Wednesday's and Friday's.' It being Friday made me realize it might be because Uncle Steve was at home.

'Bye for now aunt.'

'Bye Phillip – look after yourself and do not worry about your father. I'll put him straight about how just because he missed out on his freedom from parental control—there is no reason for his son to.'

'Bye aunt Sue.' I replaced the receiver and slid the door open.

'Yes, I got the message Dan – who's going to the Blue comet – you and Maria?'

– 'Yep, but Sal's finishing at work and coming as well.' I felt this to be a bit tricky, seeing, since I'd already been there with Pamela—even though she said I was the chauffeur. In fact, thinking about it, Pedro the bar man was ever likely to say that her chauffeur, who wasn't a chauffeur had been to the Blue Comet when she next visited to collect payment for the Sea View! I really should've recognized how this meeting with Meila was not just a holiday boy meets girl situation.

'Count me out Dan.' 'You're not serious.'

'Yes, I am this time.' I had said it then. My tongue sort of took over.

'What'll I tell Sal, and there was I looking after your interests Phil—even got you a partner. Don't tell me you're going steady after one date with Pamela?' I lied.

'Just need an early night after looking after your customers on the Downs, that's all.' That is what can happen when you're head over heels in love. You prioritize your options quite selfishly.

'You'll manage Dan,' I said.

Chapter 23

THE SATURDAY OF THE beach barbecue started, sunny, but at midday rain swept on to the beach from seawards. Deck chairs were left abandoned on the beach. A queue started forming by the cliff railway, but there were still swimmers. It's said the sea water feels warmer when it rains. Dan who'd arranged to work on the beach until mid –day with permission from Bill was with me stacking chairs. Dan's practiced eye evaluated the demand for deck chairs along the promenade when the rain started and his decision was that one row could be removed and re-stacked before we took a lunch break. This could be counter-productive, because should the rain stop, demand for deck chairs could pick up again in the afternoon and out they would go.

'Not looking good for the barbecue Dan,' I said.

'The forecasts okay Phil, It's supposed to clear, before this evening. Anyhow I finish at twelve thirty. I've squared it with Bill you can come out on Sea

Spray to Thanet—help set up the barbecue.'

'That's okay by me,' I said.

On previous occasions it was me who stood in for Dan covering the Downs. As newest recruit decisions tended to be made over my head. Ian covered for Dan today.

I was beginning to wish I had not suggested lighting the barbecue two hours early, to allow it to get heated. The party was due to start after working hours, but with the rain the demand for deck chairs was likely to fall away. My main concern was getting back in time to meet Meila outside the Blue Comet.

I signed off in the Beach Inspector's office at two, which had been arranged earlier.

Sea Spray was alongside the landing stage. A sixteen foot Orkney style open launch with a ten horse power diesel. It was secured to the side opposite to where pedalos, and rafts were hired out.

Dan was talking with Malk when I walked up the ramp and across to where they were standing. Malk, I guessed was nearer to fifty then forty, clean shaven, but once black hair now greying and cut short. Skin blackened by daily exposure to wind and sun. He wore cutaway fraying jeans, a wide leather belt, with a sheath knife, canvas deck shoes and a white vest which was usually spattered with spots of diesel oil as it was today.

'The pump starts up in the bilges when the water level rises. It's been replaced this season, Danny boy. You should have no problems,' said Malk. He owned and ran Sea Spray, the ferry, and the boat beach operation of pedalos and rafts together with Antonio, who was said to have met up with Malk on a North Sea oil rig. Dan was familiar with Sea Spray, he told me. After work he would sometimes hitch a lift across to Cliff Side, which was above Blackberry Cove. Dan pointed out the roof of Malk's summer beach home to me when in the bar. Sea Spray was used to tow the pedalos, between Babbacombe and Blackberry Cove where they were kept overnight in a small harbour.

'I can bring Sea Spray back by six for you to take your party out.' The Landing Stage will be there when you go, but you'll need to tie up next to the diving board when you come back from the Barbie.' I heard Malk say to Dan. The Landing stage was winched up the beach at the end of the day, but when the tide came in there were concrete platforms with ring bolts next to the diving platforms on the far side of the beach. In calm summer seas it was safe to take a small boat like Sea Spray in under the cliffs and tie up. It meant a short walk along a cliff path to get back on to the promenade. How many are there?'

'Ten,' said Dan.

'Bit of a squeeze. Comfortably seat seven. A couple may have to sit on the deck in front of the engine. He pointed to the space in front of the engine housing. Sea Spray was already started. The exhaust made a healthy popping sound.

'Got the cash?' 'Fifty?' asked Dan

'Yep, special concession for beach workers.'

Dan reached in his back pocket and counted out five ten-pound notes before handing them to Malk. We'd all paid ten pounds to Dan. But no profit in it for him after he'd paid out for baps, sausages, and bananas. Baked bananas on baps or beans being the vegetarian option. Don't ask me how Dan decided on bananas and baked beans. Ingrid said she could supply large bottles of Coke and lemonade at cost plus a catering size of baked beans. We deck chair attendants contributed a fiver each for bottles of white wine and Bacardi from the local discount store.

'You can run Sea Spray, gently mind, on to the sand when you arrive at the island. One of you take the painter up the beach, and the stern line while the other gets your barbie kit out,' Malk said pointing to the boxes behind the engine. Run her out about twenty feet to anchor and then swim ashore. You'll have two lines ashore. You've done this off Blackberry Cove Dan, you know the score. Dan looked a bit peeved.

'I took a party out last year Malk.'

'No harm going through the drill again,' said Malk. Dan's remark not putting him off his stride.

'Next time you go out with your passengers remember the tide will be in full flow you'll need to let out most of the anchor rope –but make shore you take bow and stern line ashore. Sand around Thanet doesn't always hold an anchor too well. Just switch the engine off. No need to switch it off at the fuel tank as you've seen me do at night. You should then have no trouble re-starting. Think that's about it.' Malk walked across to the booking office kiosk on the landing stage and returned with a card. Here's my mobile number, if there're any problems.

'That's great Malk. We'll be on our way then,' said Dan.

we both lowered ourselves from the platform onto the stern of the boat. Malk lifted the bow line off the bollard, coiled it and threw it back aboard. Pushed the bow seawards and did the same with the stern line. Dan simultaneously pushed the tiller across while gently but consistently increasing the engine speed. I immediately got the feeling that Dan was an expert at handling Sea Spray. I enjoyed looking back at the view of the beach and surrounding red cliffs, before this disappeared when we rounded the promontory of Thanet Island.

It was calm on this side, of the island, because there was a strong off shore breeze. I would say Dan followed Malk's instructions to the letter. He was the one who stripped to his swim shorts and swam ashore with the stern line, while I found a stout weathered tree stump for the bow line, and a heavy rock to wrap the stern line around. It was then a case of collecting a stash of pebbles and rocks to make an oven wall for the metal grid to go on—well up the beach away from the incoming tide. I suggested leaving spaces in the oven wall to help generate a draught. We stayed for twenty minutes after lighting meths on charcoal to ensure bricks were really heating up. Dan swam out and hoisted the anchor up and re-started the engine. I pulled Sea Spray into the beach. It was nearly four when we arrived back at the landing stage on Babbacombe Beach. I ran to the cliff railway and just got aboard before the doors closed. It was cutting it all too fine for meeting Meila outside the Blue Comet at five. The last thing I wanted to happen was to arrive after five o'clock.

Chapter 24

I FELT BETTER AFTER I was out of my beach togs showered, and shaved. I looked at my mobile and it said four thirty-five. A pair of Jeans, over swim shorts plus Tee shirt and trainers and I was ready. I returned to the flat from the landing to grab a towel, which I placed scarf like around my neck, but then neatly folded it into a roll before stepping outside. Personal presentation now at a heightened level. I walked along the Downs towards the Blue Comet. There was relief that the phone now said ten to five. I wasn't going to be late.

I was waiting outside the Blue Comet for a few minutes and Meila arrived in a tee shirt, jeans, and trainers almost identical to mine, save that the trainers had pink flashes down the sides.

'We're twins,'

'That's a good sign isn't?' The holding of hands as we walked toward the beach road and the smiles from Meila made the world very all right, I remember. We walked past the water trough at the top of the beach path. The angel above had a bunch of pink wild thrift picked by a child and placed in its outstretched hand. The rail car was now stopped and run back from the station door to prevent vandals breaking in overnight.

'I can show you where I sketched,' I said. The road to the beach was still home to meandering visitors and we could avoid them.

'We can go through the trees and around the barrier and get back on to the beach path. I can show you where I used to stand with an easel. Meila's eyes lit up.

'I would like that. Let's live dangerously.'

'It's not that dangerous. There've been no more rockfalls, as far as I know. I expect that they will clear away the rubble and open the path again,' I said.

I held Meila's hand and led her away from the path through the ivy carpeted ground beneath the trees, which took us around the blocked entrance and back on to the path. The birds were chattering and you could still hear the occasional car the other side of the now closed railway line. The path was made up of gravel and protruding rocks intermingled with the red mud and roots that surfaced from mainly fir trees that clung to the sloped cliff side.

We stopped holding hands, and selected where to walk among the uneven path.

'We could swim on the beach after work,' I said. 'That's if you'd like to.'

'Yes, but not during the day. There are too many people. It's not my scene Phill-ip. I do like swimming though. That would be cool.' We rounded a corner where there was a circular railing in front of a bench. This made a space like a miniature Amphitheatre, which overlooked Babbacombe Bay below.

'I used to set up an easel here with a part finished sketch of the trees below with the sea as a back drop. When visitors walked by either up or down from the beach they might stop and look and then I would offer to do a pencil portrait.' Meila moved close and placed her arm around me. We kissed.

'I would very much like to have a sketch of yours Phill-ip. Not of me, but just one that you have done perhaps – for me? Those appealing almost plaintive eyes looked into mine before she smiled. We continued our walk to the beach. In front was a pile of rocks and rubble, but only partly on the path.

'They'll clear that away I expect, and re-open the path,' realizing that I was repeating myself.

'I have heard they set off explosives. Noise and vibration can dislodge rocks, near to falling.' We were more than halfway to the beach and the railway went over the path at this point. A concrete bridge spanned it, making it secluded and hidden. There was a bench inside, where walkers could sit and shelter from the rain or just rest. It was not pre-planned, unless subconsciously, but I took held of Meila's hand before we walked under the shade of the bridge and we embraced. I was kissing her neck before our lips met. Meila was wearing a bikini top under the tee shirt I discovered after my hand ran up her back under the tee shirt. She stepped away and we both sat on the bench. My fingers found the clip for the bikini. She continued to kiss my neck in receptive reply. The top fell away. It was Meila who removed it from under her tee shirt and placed it on the bench. This allowed me to caress a firm nipple. I held my hand around her breast in place of the bikini. Her lips moved from my neck to my ear. Tongue licking it before she kissed my lips hungrily several times. We ended with a longer kiss, which led to gentle, but insistent tongue caressing.

I wanted to go further. She drew back and placed her hand on mine beneath the tee shirt.

'I want this Phill-ip,' she said. 'I want it very much. But not here.'

'You do understand. I know it is difficult to go this far, but it is for a woman as well. I want it to be where we can make love and sleep together. There is the barbeque. Isn't there? I removed my hand from around her breast.

'I got carried away,' I said. Meila moved towards me to kiss first one cheek then the other.

'No, she whispered. I love you Phill-ip and I love you for understanding as well. Perhaps we should sit here for a little while. She smiled, but looked genuinely disappointed before turning to recover the bikini top. I saw where the bikini strap ran along her back when she lifted the tee shirt to hold the bikini back in position.

I would have liked her to remove the tee shirt completely, to help her replace the top but then she wanted to cool things down and was wanting to lower the temperature, not accelerate it.

'Can you please Phill-ip?' Her fingers held the two straps and I re-fastened the catches. I straightened the crumpled tee shirt and was rewarded by Meila turning around to kiss me. She stood up to recover her floral-patterned beach bag, which lay in the middle of the path. Hand held out from where she stood.

'All right Phill-ip?

'Of course.' I said, smiling. I stood up and held her hand. We walked out into sunlight, on the other side of the bridge.

Chapter 25

MEILA LED THE WAY out on to the pavement to the beach. She spotted Sea Spray alongside the landing stage.

'I can see Olga,' she said, and pointed to where she was standing getting ready to board. Dan could be seen holding out a hand to steady her when she stepped across on to the boat.

'Who are the two girls already in the boat at the front?'

'That's Maria and Sal. They work at Cliff Side.' Before we stepped off the promenade on to the beach there was a call and wave from Ingrid. We walked across.

'You have just made it,' she said. All valuable are to be left in restaurant. It is safest. It is small boat and then also you may leave things behind.'

'That sounds like a good idea,' said Meila.

'The others they have taken their phones, but that is their decision.'

'We won't need phones,' said Meila and smiled at me.

We followed Ingrid into the restaurant. There was a cupboard behind the counter, which she opened.

'Put them on the shelf, there,' said Ingrid pointing. I placed my phone next to Meila's.

'I expected there to be more people going to the party,' Meila said, as we walked down to the beach area.

'It is a bit restricted the boat can only take ten. There's Barry and Ian. I pointed to them. They were talking as they walked down the beach towards the Landing Stage ahead of us.

'I know Ian, but not Barry,' she said. The pebbles fell away beneath our feet as we walked down the beach. The planks on the stage were still damp in places from the earlier rain as we walked on it.

'The most senior personnel usually board last,' said Dan as

I stepped on to the thwart and held out my hands to assist Meila.

'That's right Dan.' Meila gave a mock salute as she stepped aboard.

Almost simultaneously Barry and Ian stepped from the stage on to the boat, assisting its movement away from the side with a foot push. Meila sat next to me and Ian opposite with his guitar in a canvas case at his side.

Meila smiled at me and looked relaxed and happy. Dan increased the throttle on the engine.

'Hope you are right about the barbecue heating up Phil,' he said. Dan, was stood, holding the tiller between his legs to light a cigarette.

'So do I,' I said not wanting to be seen as the one responsible, if the charcoal was not hot enough for cooking.

'Give it here Dan,' said Ian, when the lighter wouldn't light the cigarette in the breeze. Dan handed lighter and cigarette to Ian, who was able to crouch lower down and light the cigarette, before handing cigarette and lighter back to Dan.

'That doesn't mean that I condone smoking, but I'd rather feed your addiction if it makes you a safer helmsman.'

'Thanks Ian,' said Dan after taking a needed gasp on the cigarette. Meila looked to be enjoying the exchange between these two. I noticed that the tide was a little further up the beach than when we first went out to light the barbecue. It was a bit like arriving on a desert island. Dan slowed right down and the bow bit into the soft sand. It was possible to scramble over the bow and on to the beach without getting your feet wet. I caught Meila as she jumped down. Apart from Dan Meila was the last to disembark. I helped carry the boxes containing the barbecue, drinks and plastic plates and cups up the beach, while Ian and Barry secured the lines after Dan went a little way out to anchor.

I placed my hand just above the grid over the charcoal and felt a fierce heat. The charcoal was turning to that grey shade when the briquettes have matured and burnt to produce the heat necessary for grilling

Chapter 26

IAN, TOOK OVER AFTER the barbecue. It was sort of inevitable. He was the one with a guitar. The sun was still well above the sea. A cool breeze, sneaked around the island on to the sand, which caught barbecue smoke and blew it seawards. Ingrid insisted everyone filled bin liners with rubbish from the meal.

'No singing or dancing before the beach is clear of where we've been,' she insisted; this before a strum of guitar chords invited everyone to join Ian, sat on a solitary rock further up the beach.

'Hey that's really good,' said Pamela – about Ian's guitar playing as we put paper cups in the plastic bag. There had been mention of further swimming. Several of us swam out and back from the anchored boat, earlier, and others swam before the barbecue.

We, that's Meila and I went over to join the others standing in front of where Ian was playing.

A relaxed atmosphere, on the island, and sense of being away from the world, drove out feelings of embarrassment— who was watching anyway? Sand even this far up the beach was still damp, but firm to stand on. Ideal, for bare foot dancing. Annie and Olga jigged in front of Ian, to a rock number belted out on guitar—Dan allowed himself to dance with Ingrid. Barry, walked over to where Maria was left sat to one side of the rock.

Meila, clapped to the song and then stood in of me, in green bikini with a tantalizingly dance back and forth, throwing in a couple of high kicks to advertise attractiveness, as if I wasn't fully aware.

'Come on Phill-ip,' she said and reached down with both hands. I grabbed hold of Meila's hand and pushed myself away from the beach. Ian, at that moment, slowed the rhythm right down and sort of accompanied a guitar beat to a vocal humming and dancing to Stranger on the Shore. I held Meila in my arms. Hair, fell across my neck when we were close. Hair, still damp from when we went swimming. Meila, the more powerful and effective swimmer, but I realized this was a moment go hold her close. When Ian stopped playing, we sat on the sand arms around each other.

Barry, I saw was talking to Maria. She looked up and smiled at him – a virtual stranger among the group of us, who already knew each other. Perhaps, Maria felt left out by easy familiarity of others.

'I can't sing.' called out Ian, which was a lie, I thought. 'Who can sing?'

'Annie you can sing,' said Ingrid. I hear you sing in the kitchen.' I was embarrassed for Annie at that moment. We may all sing in the shower or when we feel that no one else is listening. What I didn't know was that Annie belonged to a group and was the lead girl singer. Quite misdirected by Ingrid saying that she sang in the kitchen of the restaurant. Perhaps the others were aware of how good she was? The diminutive Annie stepped out from the group and walked over to stand next to Ian.

Her voice seemed to fill the beach and everyone stopped talking to listen. There was applause immediately on finishing the song. I realized afterwards that Annie's captivating singing knocked Dan back. His comedy turn was planned for the evening's entertainment.

There was no real competition until Annie started singing. There were cries of 'more, more from our small group Annie continued with a medley of songs. Ian contributed with a background of guitar chords, mostly at the beginning and end of each snippet of song. Each few bars made you want to hear the whole song sung by Annie. We all clapped enthusiastically at the end.

'More, more,' called out Barry, but Annie bowed a couple

of times and was embraced by Olga when she returned to the watching group. Ian sang the first verse from a Beach Boys song, — 'We came on the sloop John B my grand pappy and me,' but broke off to make an announcement, having caught our attention.

'And now for the main act of the evening.' Ian strummed his guitar for several seconds to highlight the event. There were hurricane lights hung at the back of an open cave. A backdrop for Dan to stand to perform his comedy act. We followed Ian and Dan into the sandy alcove. Dan looked chastened by the performance Annie gave. A sort of haunted look in his eyes. None of us had heard any of his material.

It was Ian who suggested he broke the ice in front of people he knew. Now this seemed less of a of a good idea. The others were crowding around Annie, congratulating her on her singing. In this small party she'd found stardom. I didn't think she would be seen as the quiet retiring kitchen assistant we imagined her to be. Annie was a hard act for Dan to follow. He went across to speak to Ian.

Quite a lengthy conversation. It appeared that Dan was less keen to stand in front of an audience. His light no longer as bright after such a stellar performance. The confidant joviality replaced by withdrawal and a switch away from confidence and assurance. Not a good place for a comedian to be about to stand in front of an audience.

Particularly an audience who would've been happy for Annie and Ian to continue until the party ended and we all left the island on Sea Spray.

'Thanks Annie,' Dan said, 'that was some real neat singing.

Good evening everyone. I once went to Ozz – some of you may know that,' Dan turned to face us. We were sitting on the dry sand of the cave floor. A strum of the guitar followed.

'Really? That's already surprised us,' said Ian, who was probably expecting to introduce the act anyway.

'Tell, do tell us more – do.' Ian, strummed his guitar once

118

again to put an introductory note into the act. Ian's comment was probably not part of the act, but it got the first laugh from the audience with our experiences of Dan's forever talking about his time in Ozz.

'I got off the plane and went over to immigration. They asked me at immigration why I'd decided to leave the old country. I said my Mate Ben moved to Ozz and it turned his world upside down.' Dan paused expecting a laugh from the Australian analogy. One or two of us caught on, but too late for good effect.

'There was a tall and a short customs officer. The short one unzipped my grip, while he looked straight at me and then zipped it up again. Perhaps this action gave him access to my mind through looking into my eyes, without having to rummage inside it, I don't know.' There was a bubble of appreciation from the audience.' The idea that a customs officer might have a sense of humour was humorous, but didn't get that much of a response.

"What do you do?" The shorter one of the two immigration officers asked

"I'm an engineer."

"You're welcome here we're always wanting bridges built." "Not all the way back to the old country though,' said the other one."

"I'm not that kind of engineer. I work on motor cars."

"Like the ones with kangaroo petrol in their tanks you mean?"

"Yes, could be," I said.

"Don't expect to see kangaroos here in the streets unless you've been drinking though," the tall one said.

'They waved me through,' Dan continued 'and I caught a cab to the youth hostel. The guy on the reception desk asked if I'd got a criminal record. I didn't think you still needed one to get in, I said. This got a murmur of disapproval from one or two. There was a distinct lack of original material. It was as if

119

Dan just strung a few jokes about Australians together.

"Are you married?" Asked the guy, behind the reception desk.

"No, I said – too young for that, I replied,' continued Dan.

"There you go I was talking to my wife only last week. In a casual sort of way, I told her I never want to be left in a vegetative state dependent, in old age, on fluids from a bottle.

'Do you know what she did?"

"No, what did she do? I asked," said Dan.

"She got up from her chair unplugged the TV—went to the refrigerator and chucked all my cans of Fosters out." This drew a few laughs. Ian came in with a guitar number and there was some polite clapping, while several gathered around Annie, to congratulate her on her impromptu singing. I looked back down the beach and much of the sand was enveloped in the ink black of an incoming tide.

The next wave from the incoming tide surged higher and the glow from the remaining charcoal disappeared into a sizzle of smoke and steam. It was like a signal. We walked away from the cave area with Dan carrying the hurricane lamps. Unlike the mainland beach the island had a stretch of brown sand, now being covered by the tide. Sea Spray was a good thirty feet from the shore. Anchored, but now also held by a line running ashore tied to a tree stump.

'Fancy swimming out Phil,' said Dan from further up the beach; to hoist the anchor?'

'I'll race you,' said Pamela, who was lay on the sand next to me.

I was about to refuse. Saying that I didn't know how to start the engine. I had to ditch my wimpy excuse after this challenge.

'Just hoist the anchor and I'll pull Sea Spray in from here,' said Dan with a smirk on his face.

'No need to start the engine Phil.' There was never any doubt who would reach the boat first. Pamela's racing crawl meant she was already on the ladder at the boat's side before I was half way out.

'Sometime—maybe, perhaps I'll show you how to swim more like a fish than a crab,' she said laughing as I reached to grab hold of the ladder. Meila followed me on to the foredeck. 'What shall I do?' she asked. The nylon anchor line was running almost directly to the sea be

'I may need your muscle power to get the anchor free.' 'Would it be useful if I held you?'

'Be useful? Most definitely,' I said as I leant forward to haul the rope in. I nearly regretted the offer when Meila's cold fingers and hands wrapped themselves around my waist. I shivered

'Don't you like being held by me, any longer then?' 'Your hands are like blocks of ice.'

'Ah, cold hands warm heart, isn't that what they say?'

I did then get several kisses across my shoulders. I was beyond worrying about the awareness of our closeness from those on the beach.

'Is this any help?' she asked. I smiled back Meila knew the answer.

It took both hands to get sufficient purchase and break the anchor from the sea bed.

But afterwards it was straightforward. The bow started to turn. Dan and Ian dragged Sea Spray shoreward. Everyone was waiting at the water's edge when the bow buried itself into the sand. Already the beach sand had shrunk to half its size. Dan boarded over the bow and I helped take on belongings like bags and towels. Ingrid insisted the grid from the barbecue was taken off the island along with a black bag of rubbish.

The boat was swung sideways to the beach. It was Olga and Sal who splashed water at those of us already sat on thwarts as others climbed aboard.

'Stop that,' called out Dan. If water gets in the engine, we could be here all night.' The engine cover was open. No engines take kindly to salt water at the best of times. Dan had been given strict instructions on how to start and run it by Malk.

Maria was with Annie and Olga in the bow. The drinks had made an impression on them judging by the laughter coming from where they were seated. An offshore breeze caught us as Sea Spray came around from the shelter of the island. Houses made visible by pinpricks of lights now beginning to show high up in the cliffs. We were in deep water because the beach ended abruptly about five metres out. The distance greater than when we set out due to the risen tide. The engine was at full throttle for about three minutes. Dan reduced speed and it was then that there were shrieks from Maria, Annie and Olga sat in the bow.

'The floor's starting to float.' I recognized Annie's voice above the engine noise.

'We're flooding,' from Olga and from Maria – 'I can't swim.' The bow lurched downwards. The added weight of those sat in the bow probably accelerating the inward flow of water. Dan stopped the engine. There were life belts around the engine housing, but no one was wearing a life jacket.

We couldn't have been more than ten metres from Babbacombe beach, but that wasn't going to help a non-swimmer. The bow settled first and I could see the water was above their waists. Within seconds the boat slipped from under us. 'Maria,' called Dan, but there was no reply. He swam forward and downwards into the water. I tried the same, but lost my breath and surfaced almost immediately. It was Barry's voice that called out.

'I've got her.' He was holding Maria with his arm in the rescue position, about fifteen feet away. There was still some daylight. She was gulping out water, to start with. 'I'll get her to the beach,' Barry said, breathlessly. Dan had the presence of mind to call out everyone's name. We all answered back, as if in reply to a school register. Everyone, that is except Maria.

Several, including Meila and Ingrid then swam toward the shore. Barry a trained lifeguard back kicked his legs to propel the two of them toward the shore. Everyone made it to the beach before Barry. Several of us stood almost with the water to our necks, waiting for him to make it with Maria. She appeared unconscious We carried her up on to the beach and laid her limp body gently on to the pebbles.

Chapter 27

MARIA WAS PLACED IN the recovery position. The beach was deserted, save for a gull incongruously whacking a crab's claw with its beak against a pebble. Indifferent to the life and death situation we were experiencing. The click, clicking, as it tried to crack open its prize, audible, when a wave's crash stopped to sprawl on a new stretch of beach, nearby.

Barry wasted no time.

'I need your help to turn Maria on to her back,' he said.

He knelt by her side, and drew his hands back and forth to indicate we needed to turn Maria over.

'Dan, you lift from where I am here. Ian, Phil take hold of her middle and upper body will you? We lifted from the middle, while Ian held Maria's left shoulder. Barry now moved to take hold of her head to prevent it banging on to the beach, when we moved Maria from back to front.

'Right, gently does it. We lifted Maria sufficiently to roll her on to her back. A sigh was emitted when she settled. Both eyes remained closed. The sigh could be interpreted one of two ways. Barry placed his ear to mouth and nose only momentarily, to check breathing. Ingrid already held Maria's wrist. She looked up at Barry

'I cannot feel, the movement in the wrist. There is nothing moving.' He checked that there were no obstructions in her mouth before giving mouth to mouth resuscitation. He looked down to spot movement from her chest. The now faltering sunlight caught on the dripping clamminess of Maria's tee shirt. Barry followed with compressions to the chest It was as if we'd all been stabbed by silence. After three or four compressions Maria coughed and gulped out water. Ingrid went and placed an arm around her shoulders and helped her into a sitting position. It was Annie who knelt next to Ingrid.

'Maria you're going to be all right now,' she said. We're safe on the beach.'

Maria spluttered with a hand over her mouth before reaching to rub her eyes, which blinked open to see our anxious faces looking down.

'I can, I can remember – going under and seeing light through bubbling water –hands under my arms,' she said taking in gulps of air like a person who has just run in a race.

'I must have blanked out after that.'

Relief spread through the group. Most of us were in swim suits, which meant clothing towels, shoes, bags – everything was lost. Ingrid was dripping in a tee shirt and shorts. Maria now supported herself with hands placed on the beach behind. Ingrid reached inside her tee shirt and hoisted out a pendant chain, with a key attached. 'It's lucky I keep café key with me. I will first call an ambulance and we can have a hot drink. You will soon be all right Maria.' Ingrid slapped her back, disconcertingly, which set Maria off into a coughing fit—then she was off up the beach to the café. Maria reached back on the sand again with her hands and lifted her knees in preparation to getting up.

'Are you okay, Marie?' asked Annie. Maria obviously wanted to get on to her feet and was assisted up by Barry and Annie.

'I'm all right now,' she said, 'thanks to you Barry,' and instinctively kissed him on the cheek. Barry modestly said,

'It's just my job,'

'Will you be able to walk Marie?' asked Annie

'Best not to,' said Barry. 'Here Dan.' He crossed over his hands and arms.

'A fireman's lift is the way to go. Dan walked over and did the same and they clasped each other's wrists to make a seat. 'I feel all right now,' said Maria.'

Maybe not wanting to be carried.

'It's perhaps best not to walk just now Maria, said Annie.'

'But It's a long way to be carried from here to the café, isn't it?' She replied.

'No problem,' said Barry. We'll carry you for ten paces and then It'll be Phil's and Ian's turn. It'll be a relay. Heck we've got some muscle power here. Let's use it.' There was some giggling from Maria, when they stumbled on the pebbles. Barry counted each step up to ten.

'Phil, Ian it's your turn.' Maria nimbly slipped back down on to the pebbles, in a way which suggested that she was more than capable of walking, but was resigned perhaps to this lift from the beach by four deck chair attendants. Ian and myself were more like the skinny guys having sand kicked in their face, by the beach strong guys.

It did mean our fireman's lift technique could've easily seen Maria dropped, rather than lifted—a much less muscular rendition of a fireman's lift than Barry and Dan's. The others went on with to the Café. Maria resigned to being given help by the four of us. It is fair to say that we were all now elated that Maria was recovered after the near drowning and not too shocked by the ordeal.

It could have ended so differently without Barry's immediate life guard response, which brought her back to the surface and for his recent resuscitating abilities. When we reached the café, I said to Meila that I wished I could've played a more significant role.

'Why are you worrying? it is his job to save lives,' she said. I was surprised that Meila didn't seem that much concerned about Sea Spray sinking on the way back from the island and that Maria nearly drowned.

Chapter 28

'WHY AM I HERE?' I was lay across a couch type bed in a brightly lit office. I moved my legs to the floor, rubbing my eyes.

'Why are you here? you ask. You were found jabbering nonsense sprawled on a park bench by police officers. You were disconnected with the world. You are here to be re-connected.'

'I'm not a light bulb that goes in a light socket.'

'Phew that's progress – you are answering and asking questions. Do you realize you've been talking non-stop since you were brought in—even after they shut you down for the night?'

'Shut me down. Why am I here now – there's nothing wrong with me?'

'You're under observation. You were in a bad way when the police brought you in on Saturday. We need to know what caused you to be how you were then. Why? How did you end up on a park bench? Were you drinking? Had you been with other people earlier?'

'I don't remember the park bench. I remember being in a boat—a boat that sank.'

'Ah, we're getting somewhere. You are Phillip Norton. Is that correct?'

'Yes, I am. You know my name'

– 'Only because you kept shouting, I'm Phillip Norton and I live in a flat.'

'I said that?'

'Yes, that's all anyone could get out of you. It was robotic, as if you were trying to hang on to your identity—do you have that problem now. Can you relate to what I'm saying now?' My eyes focused on the desk where this tall dark suited man was standing. Hands lent forward on the desk and turned towards me. I just noticed that his nose was red, almost bulbous. This can occur where a person is a quite heavy drinker was what went through my mind. The name sign on his desk was angled away from me. I answered his question.

'Yes, and no. Yes, that I know my name, but no that I don't understand what happened. It's beginning to come back. I remember yesterday or some of it up until I left the beach.'

'What were you doing on the beach?'

'I was at a party with a group of people – we barbecued we danced and on the way, back the boat sank. It sank and Maria couldn't swim.'

'What happened then?' 'She was rescued by Barry.'

'And Barry is?'

'The lifeguard. Yes, Barry's the lifeguard. It was only he who could rescue Maria. I felt helpless—but we got ashore. He revived Maria. We went to the café. I walked from the beach. That's all I can remember. I think. I think that's what happened, but afterwards. I should've returned to my flat in Acacia Avenue.'

'That explains your mentioning, well more than mentioning the flat.

And saying over and over— "I'm Phillip Norton" and I live in a flat. Why do you speak so fast? Do you normally speak so fast?'

'I don't know! I said, getting irritated by the questioning. By now I'd realized this must be a doctor's consulting room. The inside of my mouth like orange peel dried out from a previous day. I didn't remember how I came to be in the office. It's how I speak I was saying to myself I'm still the same person. Why am I here and in this room? I was still wearing the clothes from the party. I remembered the tee shirt crinkly from the salt water, but which dried when we sat around the electric fire in the café. My khaki beach trousers were fresh ones, which we'd, that's Dan and me acquired from lockers in the Inspector's office. Ingrid phoned Bill to tell him that the boat sank. He drove the women from the party home. I'd been left with Dan and his concerns about what Malk would say about the boat sinking. The three of us sat in chairs around the electric fire by the mantelpiece in the café. Ian then reassuring him.

'Look Dan there was a fault. The pump must've stopped working. You didn't hit a rock or anything. The water just started coming in. It's nearly high tide now, by tomorrow it'll be visible and we'll be able to get to it when the tides out. Malk will re-float it and drag it in with the winch.' This reassured Dan. Meila, was in good spirits, I remember before leaving. We'd parted when the women all got a lift from the beach in the cafeteria. I kicked myself for not arranging another date. I remembered Ingrid walking out from the kitchen and saying 'I'm locking up now. Dan and Ian left on their bikes ahead of me.

'I'm not aware that I'm speaking faster than normal. I can remember that I started walking back from the beach. The last thing I remember was arriving at the top of the cliff road on my own.' I said to what I presumed now to be a doctor.

'Have you previously experienced black outs or episodic periods when you've lost consciousness?'

'No,' I said. 'Only once when my head was knocked against a wall at school. I came to in a pool of blood, but the nurse just wrapped a bandage around my head and I returned to the class room. There didn't appear to be any after effects.'

'It could be related.'

'All those years ago?'

'It could've created a weakness, but head injuries are not in my field of expertise.' He'd moved forward from behind his desk while we were talking and was sitting in one of the two patient chairs. He got up and moved the other one to the other side of the desk and beckoned for me to sit there. I sat opposite in the chair.

What is that field?' I'm a consultant psychiatrist. There

was a plinth like sign on his desk that said Dr Trevor Taylor. The layman, like me, assumed the title Doctor meant everyday medical practitioner. A chill went through me when he said psychiatrist.

When he next spoke, everything had new meaning. 'You're being kept under observation. I would like to book

you in for an ECG scan. Do you have relatives nearby. Do you live at home?'

'No, I rent a flat. My home is in Hertford. 'You're a seasonal worker.'

'Yes.'

'We'd like to keep you here until this afternoon. Is there someone we can contact.'

'My employer, perhaps,' I said. 'Torbay Council.

I don't have any relatives near and I'm feeling okay now.'

'Right, we can get the details up online and contact them. If you're happy for us to do that?'

'Yes, if you would,' I said. I was dazed, but otherwise feeling okay.

'There's a canteen on the next floor down, which will give you coffee and breakfast,' he said. Dr Trevor rose to his feet after several light taps on the door. It opened.

'Helen,' A white coated, fair-haired woman, holding a clip board entered.

'Just at the right time.' This is Mr Phillip Norton. He's been with us over the weekend. This sounded strange. My thoughts were about Saturday.

'What day is it I asked?'

It's Monday morning,' said the fair-haired, youngish woman, in a way that implied everyone should know. I realized then that I must have been unconscious or asleep through Saturday and Sunday. Dr Trevor returned to his desk and picked up a blue file handing it to her.

'Phillip this is Doctor Carter. I stood up. She smiled and shook my hand.

'Pleased to meet you Phillip,' she said. 'We would like you to have an ECG scan and I'll need to take your blood pressure, Phillip. If you'd like to come with me.'

Doctor Trevor seemed to undergo a personality change when Doctor Helen Carter arrived and was now almost pleasant.

'You'll be able to leave hospital later today, I expect Phillip. We'd like you to make an appointment for next week. Just a follow up.' He came out from behind his desk and shook my hand before we left. Doctor's consulting rooms are like interview rooms. Both parties trying to get a measure of the other. Where Doctor Carter's handshake was surprisingly firm, Doctor Trevor's was brisk and perfunctory. It said –

"I've got more important things to do and need to move on."

We left this zone through double doors, which were opened by Doctor Carter punching in a code. We entered Zone A, which led to a large seated reception area.

'Just sit down here a minute Phillip.' I did as I was asked. Doctor Carter went to the reception area where she talked to a ward sister and the receptionist before returning.

'I've organized at reception for you to be issued with a breakfast voucher. I would like you to have an electrocardiograph test and a test for blood pressure—but afterwards. The cafeterias through the next set of doors down the corridor—you will see the sign.

– 'Oh, yes,' she smiled at me – 'by the way there is someone who knows you there. She was a patient of mine earlier. She asked how you were and said she would wait.

I said I was scheduled to see you next.' She smiled, in a way that made me believe it was Meila.

'Really,' I said.

Chapter 29

I DIDN'T IMMEDIATELY SEE Maria. Perhaps because I was hoping to see Meila. The cafeteria was in a kind of island set back from a wide expanse of doors that led to offices and treatment rooms. A circular reception desk on the far side picked out by tall palm plants either side dominated the middle-left wall. The lift door near a curling stairway opened, which revealed a nurse and patient in a wheel chair.

After the doors closed, I looked away and saw Maria, sat on a table on the outer edge of the cafeteria. Her long hair plaited and pinned up at the back, gave an Italian look. She held a cup in her hands and was viewing the flow of subtitles on the TV screen positioned on the opposite wall. She must have sensed my approach, because she put down the cup and turned.

'Hi,' I said. 'Dr Carter said you were here.' She smiled pleased perhaps to meet someone she knew in the isolating environment of the hospital. She could see I was holding a voucher in my hand.

'I'll just get in the queue – be back in a minute.' The queue now shortened to the carpeted section within the seating area. The table Maria was sat on came into view by the time I reached the serving area. The wall screen TV was showing a holiday property programme. The flat roofed villas made me guess that it might be somewhere in Spain. The caption underneath displayed the conversation between the programme presenter and a prospective holiday couple. "No more grey sullen skies in Winter. You can say goodbye to high heating bills." These words flowed across the screen. The couple were both wide eyed when they smiled at the camera. I could do with less heat and more air in the cafeteria. I held out the voucher to the assistant in a white cap and green overall. She took it and put it on the steel strip behind boxes filled with beans, sausages, tomatoes, trays of bacon and fried eggs.

She crossed it through with a ball point.

'Tea, coffee, glass of orange or milk, scrambled egg on toast, bacon, egg, beans sausage or just cereals?' She looked enquiringly at me.

'Orange, bacon egg and tomatoes please,' I said. She pointed at the fruit juice cartons in the cabinet on the side and picked up a plate in a gloved hand.

'You'll need to hand this over at the pay desk,' and passed the crossed voucher back to me.

'It's very hot,' she said with a smile and placed the breakfast plate on to the tray. I slid it along the metal strips towards the cashier. After handing the voucher over I returned to where Maria was sitting

'Thanks for waiting, Maria,' I said and placed the tray on the table with my back to the TV screen.

'I was in Out Patients,' she said. An appointment was made for me to see Dr Carter. She asked about the boat accident and the barbeque. I said that it was organized by some of the deck chair attendants and then she mentioned your name. That you were in the hospital and could I wait, while you were given a blood pressure check.'

'I've still got to have that—after breakfast. And then rather unkindly, I said,

'You needn't've. It is just routine.' I didn't mention the episode after I left the beach. That, I was found incoherent on a park bench. Thinking back the police could perhaps have decided I was the worse the wear from drink. The hospital decided otherwise, but after an ECG scan and blood pressure check I was hopeful that they would arrive at the same conclusion as the police. I didn't tell Maria about any of this.

'No, I wanted to see you anyway Phil. Eat your breakfast before it gets cold,'

'What about you?' I said picking up the knife and fork. It's eleven o'clock – I ate before I came here. My appointment was for ten,'

'With Dr Carter?'

'Yes.' I noted the penciled eyebrows and the pinkish lipstick. The cluster of freckles either side of her eyes, which intriguingly moved together when she smiled. I tore open first one sachet of ketchup and squeezed the contents on to the bacon and then the other. She screwed up her nose. Obviously, no fan of tomato ketchup.

'It never shines like that when I'm there,' she said. I turned and saw on the screen a blue expanse of water and a white walled cottage.

'It's Galway Bay.'

It is very pretty,' I said, 'but I guess you're here because there're more visitors and more going on.'

'Yes and no.' I'm here to find out more about Alfie. But I need work to get by. You know employers see us Irish girls, as from a quaint Irish village, where all we do is work in pubs or cafes and help with the potato harvest.'

'That's an old-fashioned stereotype,' I said.

'You'd be surprised then if I told you that the manager's first words at The Cliff Side were — "you'll be used to working behind the bar then—won't you?" I swallowed my mouthful of egg and bacon before replying.

'He perhaps didn't mean it like that,' I continued.

'Huh, I don't know about that. Anyway, I came to pay my respects to Alfie. He was an elder brother, but he looked out for after me when our step parents left for Australia.'

'They walked out then?'

'No, but I had just finished at UNI and for them they must've felt their days as parents were over. I didn't want to go to Aus. I could've, but it was Alfie who let me stay at his flat until I got a position with Children in Need. I went to Africa shortly after he started work on the beach. I was so pleased for him.

He wrote and said he was really enjoying himself and that they'd kept him on for another season.' I listened to Maria as I ate my breakfast and considered her life already to have been more exciting than mine to date.

I'd been out with Meila twice and was already tied to that mast of exclusive love for her. I envied Dan, only later, who metaphorically found plenty of pebbles on the beach— the girlfriend variety, but was able to move on. I never considered until later that it was Maria who showed concern for my well-being. Maria now the one waiting for me after the shock of the boat sinking. Though she was the one who'd nearly drowned.

'He was so organized,' she continued. He'd been cutting the grass in the churchyard and now he's buried there.' Her eyes moistened, as she spoke, but she continued.

'I was going to return to Ireland, but then I met with the police and they gave me the few belongings that Alfie left, including a diary. I do not believe they looked at it thoroughly. I found a note in the cover, which Alfie must have written in rough. He wasn't a confident letter writer. I remember he prepared letters in rough several times before he a committed them to paper and envelope.

Four people sat on the table next to us. While we'd been talking a couple, who held Coke cans stopped to watch the TV nearby. We were a bit in the public eye.

'I'd rather not talk about it here Phil, but you need to know Sea View isn't the sleepy holiday hotel it appears to be. Could you meet me after at the Cliffside one evening.'

'Yes, of course.'

'There'll be a quiet corner where no one can listen in. It's about something Alfie discovered and what he was going to tell me in a letter.'

'I need to wait, Maria, to see what the Doctor says about returning to work. Would Tuesday – that's tomorrow be, okay?' I said as much to reassure myself of the day it was now. 'Can we say tomorrow about seven, is that all right? I mean if they don't keep you in.' I was beginning to feel a bit more upbeat now.

'Yes, that's great. Cliff Side is in easy walking distance.'

'We'd perhaps best exchange numbers.' Maria picked up her mobile from the table. I retrieved mine from a buttoned pocket in the khaki trousers.

'Mine's 0776943351,' she said. I typed it in and called her back so she could store my number.

Chapter 30

'YOU'VE VACUUMED AND DUSTED in the library Olga, then?'

'Yes, Mr Langridge and there are flowers on mantelpiece. I opened the top of windows as you say to clear musty smell. It is fresh and ready.

'Good the delegates should be arriving shortly. When Pamela returns from her break, I would like you to show them to the library and at four o'clock Mr

Watson would like tea and biscuits to be left outside on the long table. You know the one I mean.' The meeting was scheduled for Monday at two thirty

'Yes Mr Langridge. You not want me to serve the teas?' 'No, it's a hush hush meeting.'

'No one talks, is that what you mean?'

'No Olga it isn't, hush hush, as in secret. It's private and no one is allowed in the library, other than the twelve company members. I can't tell you anymore. Ah here's Pamela.' Pamela lifted the desk and entered the reception lobby.

'I've just explained to Olga about our special meeting in the Library for Mr Watson's company. I'm told they'll all have cards like this one.' Mr Langridge reached into the top pocket of his suit and produced a card. The name Smith and Harper printed in red, with a gold scroll type – "Purveyors of Premier Cakes" beneath. The name A N Other in the member space. He placed this in front of Pamela.

'They're only allowed upstairs to the library after handing over this card.'

'I understand Mr Langridge. You told me it was an important meeting.

I will call you if there is any problem with identity.'

'Yes, Mr Watson can then be informed.' The double door from the dining area swung open just as John Langridge finished speaking. Jim Watson walked over to the reception. There was no recognition shown between father and daughter. 'My receptionist has been instructed to admit only those with identity card,' said Mr Langridge.

'Good. I need that suitcase containing company documents from the safe John.

'Right. The safe is secured with the combination system.' He turned towards Pamela, who placed the specimen admittance card on the desk top.

'You can enter the first three numbers I gave you Pamela.' It gave the appearance that two people were always required to open the safe. The previous assistant manager was given the three other numbers. John Langridge asked him to leave after discovering that the hotel till safe frequently never contained any twenty-pound notes. He was advised by the police to mark a couple of notes with a special dye at the beginning of the day and place them in the safe box, which was for large denomination notes beneath the till. Whoever was taking the notes must have known either how to open the safe box or with a wax imprint had an extra key made. The assistant manager that day took over to give the receptionist a meal break. John Langridge was disappointed to discover that when the receptionist returned, both of his hands were stained with the violet blue dye. John made this discovery when he handed over a tray for him to take to the kitchen. He confronted him about the stained hands in the kitchen, away from the public gaze. He blustered and claimed it was ink from a hand stamp and said he was about to give his notice in anyway.

The receptionist decided to leave shortly afterwards.

Pamela was her replacement.

The safe could only be opened in the presence of both Pamela and John Langridge.

You might say it was improved security, but perhaps not in the interests of Pamela's father, who might need immediate access to the case.

'Very efficient security system on the safe John. The key. Have you the key to the library?' he asked. 'I'll be wanting to lock the door once the committee is in situ.' John Langridge handed the suitcase across the reception counter.

'Pamela the library key for Mr Watson, if you please.'

Pamela walked over to pick out the black lettered fob key marked Library from the Cabinet and returned to the reception desk Her father reached over for the key Pamela held out. She smiled.

'Thank you, young lady,' he said. She pulled a face at him for that. There was no one to see. John Langridge was talking to Olga on the far side of the desk.

'John I'll be in the library when the first members arrive.' He walked up the stairs and then on to the second landing. A taxi drew up outside in the driveway.

Headlights in heavy rain formed a webbed spray of light in the large frosted glass paneling by the patio. The front door opened and an umbrella could be heard shaken on the door mat.

A willowy woman in a pink trench coat entered holding a black leather case. Shoulder bag bouncing back and forth as she entered the hotel. The umbrella she deposited beneath the hat stand. She smoothed her hand over flowing dark hair. 'Good afternoon,' called out John. 'The rain's taken us by surprise. It's not forecast. Won't last long, I don't expect.' He always said he was surprised by the rain, even when there'd been several days of it, when he greeted new arrivals.

'Can I be of service?' He walked across, but she moved her case out of reach from his outstretched arm. She was nearly six feet tall, which dwarfed his five-foot-four.

'Have you a room booked for tonight, perhaps, madam? Is there luggage to be brought in.' This wasn't the situation, because the taxi's headlight reflection disappeared from the glass when he spoke.

'I'm here to attend a meeting.' The disdainful look suggested that a three-star hotel rating probably didn't meet with approval, but might just be acceptable to attend a meeting.

'Oh, yes, you are expected – Jim, I mean Mr Watson has asked for all members to produce card identity. She lifted the briefcase on to the desk and pressed the gold button on the front and slapped the card on to the desk.

'Thank you, that's just fine, Miss Appleguard,' he said after reading the name.

'Mr Watson is in the library. Olga, please show Miss Appleguard up to the library

'Please to follow me Miss Appleguard,' said Olga, not quite catching the name.

'Appleguard, it's Alice Appleguard.' She smiled not unpleasantly at Olga before she followed her up the flight of stairs. The rain rattled on the glass paneled roof of the breakfast room.

Chapter 31

ALEX TOMPKINS, ALIASES REMOVED, pushed the weighty key into the keyhole. The stork of the key disappeared, leaving only the key handle, which needed force to turn. He removed the key and placed it in the keyhole on the other side. The door closed and he walked by the windows to the end of the room and swung the case on to the mahogany table. He undid the strap around the middle, aligned numbers 2365 on to the dial, and pushed the catches to gain access.

He counted out twelve sausage-shaped sachets of cocaine, satisfying himself that they were unbroken before replacing them back into the case. There was a tentative knock on the door.

'Just a minute,' he said and shut the case and placed it under the chair at the head of the table. He went to open the door.

'Hi Alice.'

'Is this the only way we get to meet?' she asked.

"Fraid it is.' Alice got a perfunctory kiss after the door closed, with a smile.

'Oh, we're alone.'

'Not for long. How's Steve?' Asked Alex.

'He's marking exam papers this month. Only, surfaces occasionally.'

They walked across the room and Alice sat in the chair next to Alex's.

'Does he still have those shelves of manuals – still working on his classic car collection.

'Forever, forever, Alex. I'm the one that pays for everything.

Everything that matters. I've told him this time I'm on business for the bank here in Babbacombe. That,

I'm directing the opening of a branch for buy to let.

'By the sea,' interrupted Alex.

'Yep, by the sea.' But it keeps the meeting off the grid.' 'He knows nothing about our business association?'

'My work takes me away for days at a time. He accepts this. I admit, I usually meet my customers in better class hotels than this. That is, after I've seen bank clients.'

'He's not suspicious then?' Alex's eyes narrowed momentarily.

'No. He is oblivious to how moneys made in the real world. Steve, now accepts that people who work for banks have large bonus payments. Provided I supply cash every now and then to buy him some bit of scrap he calls a classic car he's quite happy.'

'None of your customers are clients of Loyalty Bank?'

'Not directly.'

'How do you mean, not directly?'

'The young women I sell to in hotels remark that they have clients in the banking industry. There's a good chance some of them will work for Loyalty Bank, like I do.' Alex continued with his questioning.

'Isn't it risky meeting at just any hotel? I mean hotels aren't usually overly keen to supply rooms to known call girls.'

'At the higher end of the market this is rarely a problem. Their clients make the hotel bookings and they expect to be supplied with coke and sex like they do fine dining in the restaurant. I really don't know Alex, how you can stand to stay in a joint like this.' Alex appeared not to be offended even though he was part owner of Sea View.

'Bankers call girls, not much to choose between them. They both fleece clients for as much as they can. One lends, but with high interest. The other steals their punters souls.'

'How cynical of you to say that. What does that make you Alex?'

'A facilitator for others to make money. It's a job. If I didn't supply cocaine, they'd go somewhere else.' Alice reached down to pick her briefcase up and placed it on the table.

'Is this going to be a regular place to collect from—with everyone classed as H &S company execs? That we all belong to a luxury cake company, meeting up to discuss the latest products!'

'No!' – Alex scrolled down the tablet in his hand to access race results before answering.

'Those attending are keen to feed funds into this new buy to let complex.

The next meeting will be at Rita's fashion boutique, anyhow.' Alice's eyes lit up.

'D'you want me to be a fashion model next time then?' 'No, but I want you to assist today's clients. They need mortgages from the bank to set up their holiday buy to let complexes.' His hand lightly held her waist as he continued scrolling his phone.

'The hotel fell for your area luxury cake manger's meeting wheeze then?'

Alice opened the briefcase to remove, what she called her school marm reading glasses.

'Our clients don't want any profile, that links them to the property market or drugs. Nothing that could make for questions being asked. A cake company I thought banal enough not to attract attention, Alice. I liked the word cake and coke – the proximity of name. Subtle don't you think Alice?' 'There's not a lot of subtlety about you Alex,' she said, and removed his hand, which was beginning to investigate contours below the waistline.

'I wanted to give the appearance that this meeting was a convention set by the sea for boring business types.'

'Speak for yourself,' Alice feigned being upset and sat down.

'Well, you meet plenty of that type in your line of work Alice – you know what I mean.' Alex pocketed his phone and pulled back a chair to sit next to Alice.

'How did you persuade the hotel to give a room in the

height of the season, Alex?' Alice, now seated elbows on table, flicking through files on her smart phone.

'Quite easily – really. I informed the manager, that I was undercover CID. I remain Jim Watson area manager for H&S to all outward intent. This convention billed for a meeting of H & S executives was really a means to get my team together to collate our work against crime in the area. I have a photo-copy of a Chief Inspector's identity card in a black leather wallet. It works a treat. I just held it open long enough for the words chief Inspector below the HM police insignia to be seen. It never fails to impress in the hotel trade—women especially.'

'You sexist beast Alex. But that's partly your appeal.' 'Only partly – What else?'

'I'm not saying.' The James Bond theme jingle started on Alex's phone. He stood up to answer,

'Yes.'

Walked over to the closed window curtains and discreetly opened a side curtain to look at the hotel forecourt. His clients were instructed to garage their Ferraris, Bentleys and Mercs and hire Ford Fiestas or similar from a hire company. To blend in with the mundane image of H&S company executives. Alex would let them know about the double bluff when the meeting got going. Alex liked to stay a few steps ahead.

His wealthy clients were in effect camouflaged from their non too savoury business activities. There were two Vauxhall Vectra's and a silver Ford Fiesta in the guest parking bay. He interrupted the flow of information coming via his phone.

'Yes, Mr Langridge. But how many have arrived – nine, you say. That's fine. If you would show them up right away.'

He went back to the table. Alice was brushing her long black hair in front of the mantelpiece mirror. Her business attire, a mini skirted blue suit with gold buttons. She placed the brush back in the shoulder bag

'You see I'm wearing blue for by the sea Alex,' she said, as she sat down.

'You can undo a couple of those shirt buttons. They're not going to see much of your legs.' She pouted disparagingly at him. He smiled back. But later undid a button or two, which drew attention to more than just a slim neckline.

'You've gotten ten of those gold lettered folders the bank supplies?' asked Alex.

'But of course.' Alice pushed the gold buttoned brief-case stood on the table. It flew open. Each of its concertina divisions held a slim folder. She removed the twelve folders. Placed them on the desk in front, before getting to her feet and then laying one on the table in front of each chair.

Chapter 32

VOICES COULD BE HEARD outside. 'Yes, this is the room allocated.'

'Good of you Mr Langridge, In the height of the season.' A deeper voice replied. Alice looked at Alex. 'You want me to greet them, Alex?' He slowly nodded his head.

'They've all arrived together, like some consortium. A bit worrying.'

The peremptory tap on the door sounded like an enquiry, rather than to make arrival known. Alice walked across from the mantelpiece and opened the door. John Langridge opened it further.

'Ah, Miss Appleguard,' he said.

'Mr Watson's guests have arrived,' he said. It was Alex who replied.

'Thanks John,' he called out from across the table.

'The tea and biscuits will be outside at four as requested. I've instructed Olga to knock on the door so as not to disturb you.'

'That will be all for now John.' He spoke rapidly. The raised voice implied authority.

'I quite understand. Have a good meeting.' He moved away from the door and gave a half bow before holding his hand out to direct the guests towards the library.

'Good afternoon, everyone, said Alice. All nine were now on the landing space in front of the library door. Jeff, who Alice knew from a previous meeting was at the front. A large bearded man with black rimmed glasses, whose smile suggested good humour, but was developed over the years to impress potential new clients whether of a legitimate persuasion or otherwise.

'Alice, it's so nice to see you again. Here to keep Alex in line?' asked Jeff. She smiled and said. 'I thought that was your job, Jeff.'

At the back of the group were the Jamaican brothers, Abraham, and Detroit. A grandfather came from Detroit, apparently.

The family proud of this American ancestry and the name Detroit went down the generations. Mr Lin, a Chinese gentleman at the back was a new member. Alice recognized the contingent from Bristol airport. Captain Alan Mandrake, an airline pilot now in a white linen suit was followed up by Mr Bartholomew-Smyth, the transport manager. A dapper suited man. You would not be surprised if told that he was an accountant. Alice found the name at odds with his job position. Two reception airport managers, who between them would help facilitate the smooth passage of drug consignments to Mr Bartholomew-Smyth's office for further dispatch to the Blue Comet night club. Spike, who was in the motor trade the last to enter. Not all would leave with cocaine. A quarter of Alex's outlet still went to the capital.

While Alice's back was to him Alex slipped a hand under his jacket to unclip the cover on his holstered revolver. Alice moved aside and held the door. He didn't expect trouble, but needed reassurance. Ten percent price rise on each of their consignments might elicit protest.

'Jeff!' announced Alex. Jeff stopped and took two breaths not having fully recovered from climbing the stairs.

'You devious devil Alex—executive meeting of a premier cake company. You've got the manager running round after you – eating out of your hand, already. I don't know how you do it. Where do you want us to sit then?'

'Sit where you like. It's not the Lord Mayor's banquet.' said Alex. Jeff

Ripley walked past the pictures on the wall and pulled back a chair that faced Alice's. Abraham and Detroit, who followed, removed half-length coats, and revealed webbed belts simar like a money belt around their middles. Unlike the other men not wearing suits, although instructed to by Alex. Alex raised his hand in acknowledgement to the nine who arrived. Mr Lin in a shiny blue suit, placed his case under the chair like Alex before sitting down. The first of the two women airport managers attending the meeting wore a well-tailored cerise suit, but like Alice did not rate the venue. Her nose wrinkled as did Alice's when she walked into the foyer 'I won't be staying the night here Alex,' she said.

'You know I would've booked you in at the Imperial if I knew you wanted to stay overnight Justine.' The Imperial was the premier hotel in Babbacombe. Justine, smiled at Alex.

'If it wasn't raining, and this wasn't a business meeting perhaps I might consider the offer Alex,' she said, implying she might be open to staying the night. Alice, gave her a cold stare. Alex was not available in her consideration, but she resented Justine implying she might be intending to make a move on Alex. Alice need not have worried. Bristol airport was due to go on stream shortly to bring in cocaine. Justine had a house upgrade in mind and Alex's payments were crucial. The monthly airport salary was never going to meet financial requirements for next year. It was a financial not amorous contract she was after. Her payment for assisting with the movement of drugs from Bristol airport to the Blue Comet was crucial.

'And you too Cheryl,' he quickly added. The younger of the two. In her mid-twenties, wore stone washed jeans and a double-breasted jacket, which when removed revealed a clingy primrose jumper. Her hand was spread across the table and displayed a sapphire and diamond ring on the third finger. The smile she flashed showed high-calibre feminine interest for Alex, but Alice nevertheless felt less threatened.

A silver mustached, dark suited man followed the two women and he sat next to Alice. He ran his hand through black hair re-decorated to wipe out the silver content. 'Ford Focus. Not driven one since the early days Alex.'

'Well Spike the last thing I wanted was your Silver Wraith parked outside.

By the way there's a double bluff on. The hotel manager believes I'm a Chief Inspector of police. You're plain clothes officers from the Midlands and London appraising me of what criminals are visiting the resort on crime vacation during July and August from your patches.'

'The bigger the lie the more likely you can get away with it,' said Jeff.

'You'd make a first-class Prime Minister Alex; I've always said that, wouldn't he Spike?'

'You should know Jeff – all those dumb life insurance policies you sell.'

'That'll do gentlemen,' said Alex. They were a disparate group, who were unwieldy to handle on mass. In a sense the rivalry among them a kind of holding power for Alex, though. A differing expertise within the group, but united in a thirst for further gain held unlikely personalities together. At this point playing one off against the other served no purpose. Alex said.

'Welcome everyone – Detroit.' 'Yes boss.'

'The advert for this meeting. It goes down as a listing online now, doesn't it? Detroit held his hands in the air above his lap top, which was no ordinary lap top.

'Of course. I shut it down in the lobby before I came up.

What do you take me for?'

'Just checking.' The bogus site was set up in the morning as a signal to the drug cartel members that the meeting was going ahead. The acronym H&S could be applied probably to any number of businesses or organizations. The advert was set up to confirm that the meeting was still planned, where even up to an hour before Alex might need to abandon it.

The cruise ships together with consignments arriving at Bristol airport ensured that Alex managed to supply year-round to the group. Before moving into the South West, he made a substantial donation to the local authority benevolent fund for retired officials, which helped smooth the purchase of the farm, including the purchase of council owned land adjoining the farm buildings. Alex was, perceived as the stockbroker from the city, retired from the smoke to enjoy a fortune, to all intents and purposes. The others, except Spike with his shunt repair car sales early on, Alex conceded thankfully ended were, if not pillars of the community more than just wall tiles.

The influx of funds from selling product through e-Bay with a code that directed the customer to a store pick up point for the purchase was a master stroke. The drug consignment hidden in the folds of card that covered the item would be disposed of by the uninitiated if the package went astray. The uniquely designed packaging was mainly from toy items Alex shipped in from China two years previously. He insisted that his clients, like Jeff and Spike operate the e-Bay site selling the items he provided. That when approached to supply drugs this was the only method to be used. The eBay items retailed at twenty pounds with a minimum purchase of five – maximum a hundred. The packaging size went up in volume with increased multiples of five, although only one product was ever sent.

Two out of work web illustrators designed the web sites for them and were paid pro rata, with no knowledge of the drug related nature of each site. A special code needed to be added by the drug purchaser before placing an order and making payment. The site conveniently sold out for any ordinary customer who wanted to place an order. Alex wanted to end all this and after one or two packages went astray there was the risk of being rumbled. It was decided that very shortly they would pool resources into a buy to let complex.

'Welcome to you all – Alice will now give a talk about the complexities of loan finance as applied to buy to let holiday complexes. Alex sat down.

The two women airport hostesses clapped in solidarity, for one of their own sex, when Alice rose to her feet, which made

150

the male members feel obliged to join in. Alice smiled first at Alex and then to the group around the table.

'Thank you, Alex, for your fulsome introduction. The sarcasm, that Alice was in effect not given any real introduction only appreciated by Alex and herself.

Chapter 33

Now **several folders spread** across the table were open.

'Ladies and Gentleman,' said Alice. If you look inside the folder, the middle and following pages display the Quayside Walk Complex. It's due for completion at the end of July – with occupancy planned for August. Loyalty Bank purchased the complex last year together with Babbacombe town council. A straight fifty per cent ownership stake for both parties.' Alice looked around the table to ensure everyone was attending to what was being explained.

'The bank is keen to sell on their share. That's why we're here today to get agreement on conditions and unanimous backing for the project,' butted in Alex. 'The sixty million required to buy a half share in 150 apartments is to be paid from Loyalty bank accounts with instalments over five years. Spike interrupted Alex,

'What's wrong with our own accounts?'

– 'Where's yours Spike in Chicago?' Alex smirked.

'I resent that comment. We all have bona fide businesses. What's wrong with our own bank accounts. That's what I want to know?'

'Nothing, really, but we need to obliterate connections. Loyalty, credits accounts, which won't be traced locally, said Alex. A diverse range of addresses, but your names will appear in company listings outside of Babbacombe.'

'The bank prides itself on protecting the accounts of its clients from prying local authority bodies. Perhaps I should say it is able to offer the right kind of information to satisfy their nosiness,' said Alice.

'That's not to suggest that everything is not above board. 'Absolutely,' said Alex.

'Loyalty Bank is supported at the highest level. The Government are keen to encourage smaller banking groups to challenge the supremacy of the big four. Loyalty specializes in loans to the buy to let economy. Mr Wharton's father – the local member of parliament – is on the board of directors, which is very reassuring.'

'Amounts will be taken quarterly over a three-year period,' said Alice.

'What about tenants and rent,' asked Jeff

'That's not a problem. The bank already has elderly customers, who've paid rent in advance to secure their tenancy.'

'And the online accounts that are now being used?' asked Abraham, who lay the wide belt on the table, unzipping the pouch section in which to stack the next consignment now stored in Alex's case.

'After this month I propose that we sell them as viable trading accounts with product placement. I need extra finance to make this happen. Hence the ten per cent increase.' To Alex's relief there were no questions asked about this. Alice chipped in with,

'Yes, the bank will deal with this. I've explained that as a group you want to develop your line of business in another direction. To move on to a business venture more suitable for mature clients and take advantage of demand for residential accommodation in Babbacombe.'

'Speak for yourself—mature,' said Cheryl. 'Not mature, in that sense,' said Alice.

'More well developed perhaps,' quipped Spike, who got a look from the three women.

'I will have to put up my prices at the restaurant,' said Mr Lin the restauranteur.

'In September your consignments will be coming via Bristol airport. The collection venue will continue to be at the Blue Comet Club. A courier service will be available from the airport for those who choose to use it. Alex looked across at the three from the airport. Mr Bartholomew-Smythe, the transport manager nodded his head in agreement.

Chapter 34

THE HOSPITAL MEDIC DR Carter contacted me on my mobile that Tuesday after my meeting with Maria at the hospital on the Monday.

'I've looked at the scans and tests and, they're positive. No ill-effects from your experience. How are you feeling? No dizziness or sickness? You told me that you swallowed a fair amount of water on Saturday evening when that boat sank.

Maria said she wanted to return to work and I expect you might also. That's if you don't have a headache or nausea.

'I don't seem to be suffering from any ill-effects Doctor.' I would've said this anyway, even if I wasn't feeling fit. I wanted to meet up with Meila.

'Did you sleep all right last night?' 'Yes.'

'I suggest you keep well hydrated and wear a hat in the sun. I know it sounds like instructions from a parent to a child. What were you drinking at the beach party, may I ask?'

'Mostly lager, but also Bacardi and Coke.'

'Not a good combination. Lager shandy with ice, would be better in this weather. Nothing too alcoholic. I should be advising you not to drink, but I'm being realistic. I think you're sensible enough to understand Phillip. You don't smoke?'

'That's right. I don't normally drink in the evenings save on the occasional night out.

'Good. Any headaches or dizzy spells and you need to get in touch straightaway. I see from my notes that you have an appointment for next Monday at five thirty. It's just to make sure you're fully recovered, you understand?'

'Yes, thanks Doctor for your advice and the call.

'Take it a little bit easy at work, if that's possible. Goodbye Phillip.

'Bye,' I said and switched off the phone I was planning to walk to Sea View later that morning to see Meila.

We'd exchanged mobile phone numbers and our emails, but other than confirming our meeting outside the Blue Comet we'd not been in phone contact, since the party. I pressed the start button on my lap top on a desk by the window in the flat and went to the kitchen to make a coffee. When I returned the screen was blank and the machine locked. Most of the messages I received on Outlook were from commercial firms wanting to sell me something. I still received message from the New York Times. I once went on the site and made a few comments. Now I was registered as a regular user!

At the top of the in box was a message from a Pamela Tomkins @ intergroup.com. The name Pamela immediately jumped out at me. I opened the message, but until it was there in front of my eyes it didn't fully register that it was from Meila –

Phillip, I'm worried about you. I met Maria. She has told me about your stay in hospital.

She says you are all right and back at your flat. I am so very concerned for you Phillip

Maria says she talked, to you, and you seem recovered.

Talked—but not for too long though I hope!!!

It is also very difficult to know how to write this, but I finished working at the Sea View on Monday. I am on holiday, but I may not return. I mentioned to Mr Langridge that I was moving with my mother to a new flat above mother's boutique in Paignton last week. Yesterday, he said he would be happy for me to have the rest of the week as a holiday. Am angry, because I now believe my mother arranged this. I would've told you earlier Phillip. Now I may not return to Sea View. I am at the new flat now. It is better we do not meet. I love you, Phillip. I cannot explain, but it is because I love you that we cannot meet, just now. This may not make sense, but it is not something I can explain about yet. You are still always in my thoughts and always will be.

My fondest love and kisses, Meila. xxxxxxxx

PS I hope we can meet time for a coffee in a week or so.

I read this message through again and again later in the afternoon. It was not a breaking off I tried to tell myself. It was because something had cropped up. I just had to tell myself that Meila had a good reason for us not to meet. There had to be – the "my fondest love and kisses" at the end gave reason for hope, but then what was it that Meila meant — "we cannot meet now."

There was now no point in walking along to the Sea View. Meila never mentioned she was moving flats. It seemed secretive. You need to remember I was totally immersed in the cocoon of love. You can think incessantly about a person. You can be reminded of them in the simplest of things. A colour they may like. The type of clothes they wear and you see on others, wishing the person wearing them was the one you love. A particular way she may have in speaking a word. The list is endless. Meila, I somehow believed would have a straightforward explanation.

I must have been the only person in the flat complex, it was so quiet. Everyone else working or maybe at college. I was to meet Maria at the Cliff Side, later. I can only remember how I wished I was meeting up with Meila. I really should have been grateful that Maria was in my life, but I never saw it like that then.

Chapter 35

SAL SERVED ME WITH the half I ordered,' as I stood at the bar in the Cliff Side.

'Maria's said to tell you she'll be in the snug bar.' Her eyes momentarily darted in the direction of the small bar at the end to inform me, while she completed the topping up of the half pint.

'There you are.' She placed the beer down on a bar towel.

'Are you back at work?' I realized that Maria probably told Sal about me.

'No,' but I am tomorrow.

'You are all right she asked? I mean is everything all right, you don't look that happy.' I must have looked dejected, but needed to put on a front

'I'm fine. How about you?'

'So, so—rather have a beach job today,' though, she smiled. The evening sun danced about the polished brasses. A gentle breeze, flicked the curtain in the half open window. That Tuesday was an ideal day for the beach. I liked Sal, but was still in a state of shock from Meila's message A bit closed off from the world, you might say.

The snug bar appeared empty when I walked across from the main bar. Inside to the right, hidden from immediate view sat Maria, in a navy crew necked jumper and jeans.

She smiled as I approached and put down the magazine she was reading

'How about you?' I held the sleeved glass of beer up. I'd just instinctively bought a half at the bar. Perhaps testimony to my distracted state.

'Can I get you a drink,' I asked.

'No Phil. I've just had a meal and coffee behind the bar.' I sat opposite and focused on what I remembered about when we met before.

'What have you discovered? And why are you telling me about it?' I asked I didn't want to sound indifferent. I hoped that I didn't. She slipped the magazine into a bag by the table before replying.

'It's to do with Alfie's job. You replaced him Phil.' 'Yes, I did. That was because he died of a heart attack.

'That's what the police told me. Until now there's been no reason to disagree with what they said.' I took a sip of my beer, thinking my confidence about the police releasing much information or otherwise to the public was never going to be in the superlative. Two holidaymakers in dark glasses faces red from the sun entered. The mini umbrellas in their drinks jiggled about before they placed them on the bar and sat on the bar stools. Maria lowered her voice before continuing.

'I told you that I found the letter inside the diary. There was a flap over the diary and under the flap this pencil written letter, which started with Dear M. Alfie once said jokingly that I was probably now head of the secret service. I read Criminology with Psychology at Dublin university. With Dame Judy Dench playing the role of M in a James Bond film Alfie somehow concocted a story that working for Children in Need was really a cover for my being Head of the Secret Service. It was written on paper from a shorthand notepad. He never sent the final letter to Galway and anyway I was in Africa.

He said earlier that he hoped that everything was working out for me and that he understood why I didn't want to go to Australia. He'd felt the same at the time, but his life was already in place in England. He continued, saying that he'd made a strange discovery. Apparently one of his duties was to take boxes, cool boxes he called them to the Sea View Hotel.' Maria picked up a beer mat, looked at it, before placing it back down like you might a playing card.

'Yes, I know about that – I have to do the same,' I said.

'Every Thursday and sometimes on a Tuesday the ferry

brings the boxes across from the other side of the bay. Apparently, the roads are very congested and the dairy sends them by boat. The dairy operates from the harbour side in Paignton.

'That's Phil, why you should know about this. Alfie dropped one of the empty boxes and a gap appeared near the bottom. Like a secret compartment. He said he was able to slide it open like a drawer. Inside there was a long sausage shaped indentation. He considered it to be an extra compartment to protect some product that might get damaged or that needed extra insulation, but then this white shiny powder like fine sugar came out.

Alfie said in the note that out of curiosity he dipped a finger into it and took a taste thinking it might be icing sugar. Perhaps off a cake from the dairy. It tasted medicinal, apparently, and he realized it must have leaked from something inside. The following week he managed to wheel the truck under some trees by the cliff path, Phil, before he delivered the boxes to the hotel.' I took a sip of beer before replying.

'This was quite a lengthy letter,' I said.

'Yes, with crossings out it covered four sides. Apparently, Alfie removed a full box from the trolley and knocked the lower part against a rock which caused it to slide open. Inside there was a sausage shaped plastic bag containing this white powder.'

'That would make me think drugs, straightaway,' I said.

'Alfie's from an older generation. He perhaps didn't make the connection straightaway. He apparently replaced the lower compartment and delivered the boxes as normal. He could've been writing about it to me, because he wanted someone to confide in.

At the end he said that he'd reported what he'd discovered, to the police and felt better about it. I so wish he's sent the letter.' She reached for a tissue from her bag.

'Why haven't you been to the police then?'

'Would they believe me? They never even looked at this

note.' I'm not sure they'd believe what Alfie wrote. There's no real evidence that these bags did contain drugs. Alfie may have got it all wrong.' Maria dabbed her eyes.

'Do you want me to look at the cool boxes next week? I'll be going up with the trolley. I can check it out. See if there is any truth in what Alfie wrote.

There's a CID police chief inspector staying at the hotel.'
'How do you know that?' she said raising her eyebrows.

'I listened in on a conversation between him and the manager. He's like incommunicado or undercover. It won't be like going to the local uniform police. He probably deals with criminal activity like drug smuggling. I suppose it is possible there' are people on the beach or in the ferry service who know what's happening or even getting a cut.

'I'd never thought of that. That's, of course if it is a drugs consignment going into Sea View. Perhaps that's why Alfie didn't tell Bill, the beach inspector about what he'd discovered.'

'They'll not see it as unusual your, visiting the hotel with or without the cool boxes. There's Pamela. I met her on Monday. She is worried about you Phillip.

She was with Olga, on the Downs taking a break yesterday afternoon after we'd met at the hospital.'

I didn't mention the message that I'd received that morning from Meila, but said.

'Pamela's taking a holiday from working at Sea View and has move to a new flat to help her mother.'

'You'll still be seeing her though?'

'Yes,' I said,' lying because I didn't want to accept that we'd parted at that moment or for that matter tell Maria.

'Olga kept questioning me about Dan – like was I sleeping with him now.'

'Do girls ask that sort of question?'

'They do when they want to know where they stand. Whether someone they're interested in is more than just interested, if you know what I mean.'

'Weren't you annoyed that Olga asked you directly like that 'Why?' Olga's obviously is keen on Dan. I didn't come here for a holiday romance. I came pay respects to Alfie. Now I'm trying to find out what really happened. Dan said he'd show me where they found him on the beach and I went along with that. It does seem that there could be beach involvement if there's drugs smuggling.'

'Hang on Marie. Alfie died of a heart attack according to the coroner's report, and anyway why are you confiding in me?'

'Because you took over from Alfie a few weeks ago and are separate from everyone. I decided to speak to you about this when I knew you were in the hospital at the same time as me. I feel that perhaps there are people who want everyone to believe that Alfie died normally. To just say he was a middle-aged man with a heart problem.

Remember – that time we met on the Downs. I'd already talked to the vicar at the church.

'St Mary's across from the Downs? – Where Alfie cut the grass?

'Yes. Apparently, they held a reception, a sort of wake, at the Sea View,' said Maria. 'The vicar went on to tell me how one of the guests – who stayed there said that it was a nice way to go. To be enjoying his work, and for Alfie to be called away to meet his friends and family in that other seaside in the sky, as the vicar put it. He then went on to say that he knew of a retired fireman, like Alfie, who was found slumped across his tractor, after a sudden heart attack, the engine still running. The family was comforted that he died while on the tractor actively engaged in work he enjoyed, like Alfie. Until I got Alfie's belongings and read the four-page note stashed inside the diary I went along with what everyone said. That basically Alfie died doing a job he enjoyed.'

'You'd read the note that Alfie left, before going to the bar-becue.

'Yes.'

'Have you told anyone else?' Marie looked puzzled.

'Not about the note, but I did mention to Dan that I needed to collect Alfie's belongings from the police. You told me that he'd adopted Skittles. I then went to the beach on Saturday and Dan showed me the boulder where Alfie was found face down. The coins, apparently, from the money pouch spread across the pebbles. I didn't like the attitude of the Beach Inspector. He said it was Alfie's own fault working after leaving the fire service on health grounds.

'Did he know who you were?

'No, Dan said he was just showing me where he died – not that I was his step sister. The Inspector almost spoke, as if Alfie deserved to die.'

Chapter 36

IT WAS SEVEN-FIFTEEN WEDNESDAY morning. I was early, but then the tide was still halfway up the beach and I wanted to go for a swim before the day started. The diving board, chained to the sea bed lost its purpose once the tide retreated and I wanted to immerse myself with my thoughts in the waves. A kind of cathartic escape from that message from Meila that she didn't want to see me.

There are those moments when you retrieve the experience of happiness only when looking back. This was how I felt. The breeze further out flicked spray from the wave tops before I grabbed hold of the metal ladder at the back of the diving board. A seagull took flight from the board as I clambered on to its cream painted surface. Pools of water formed around my body as I sat on this rocking platform, while the gull squawked as it reached the beach and then wheeled higher into the red sand stone cliffs above. The ferry was not due for over an hour. The gulls would then leave their rock face homes to escort the wake of the boat into the landing stage.

The beach and diving board were shadowed from direct sun, but it was early July and the South westerly wind warmed everywhere before the sun-scorched people and pebbles. I lay down to recover my breath, but then looked towards the beach. Blue, red, and yellow hire floats were stacked near to the car park. The twin hulls made of a plastic material, with molded strips for either, sitting or standing on. The surface I was sat on covered with beads of brine that gave a sort of frost like texture to the surface. I turned around to position my back against the ladder beneath the Terylene matted diving plinth above. There was no morning mist. The sun caught on the white hull and hotel like structure of a cruise liner. In contrast a super tanker farther out like a canister in the water with a flat at the stern for the crew. The price of petrol was rising at the pumps. The tanker's cargo similarly maturing in value each day it stayed at and anchor. But at the time I was more shocked at my inability to contribute much to the saving of Maria. That aftermath came back in my mind vividly while I lay on the diving board. Ingrid went to call an ambulance, but Maria said she felt all right. An ambulance, drew up in the car park after Maria's rescue. I do remember Meila leading the swim back to the shore.

Perhaps she was unaware that Maria was drowning. I was more concerned about Meila's feelings toward me than those of Maria's at the time, I remember. Sea Spray's sinking was though the lead in to subsequent discoveries. Maria was sipping tea with a blanket around her.

'We'd like to do some checks in the ambulance, 'the paramedic said.

'Pulse and heart rate,' that sort of thing. He advised Maria that she should in any event go to the doctor first thing. That was how we met up on the Monday. Although beach bags and towels went down with the boat, most of my belongings were in the cafe locker together with my phone. Ingrid having previously organized most of us into leaving valuables locked up in the restaurant. I sat next to Meila, who was like Maria wrapped in a towel sipping tea.

'It reminds me of Hong Kong. We used to swim from the boat to shore. Although not from a sinking boat,' she said. A reflection of the recent past. That was all gone. That intoxicating excitement of being with Meila gone, now that she'd messaged me.

The hooter from the railway station sounded, and woke me from my reverie about the barbecue, boat sinking and hospital visit. This signaled the railway was open for the day.

Chapter 37

I HEARD THE SPLASH of alternate paddles digging into the water. I turned from my gaze seawards toward the oncoming raft. It was Ian in a beach shirt, with orange life jacket and rolled up trousers. Visitors who hired the floats were usually in swim wear. He was crouched, legs apart plus the rapid alternate dip of the paddles, displayed a skill I'd never seen when visitors were sat on a raft, let alone stood.

'It's you Phil.' Ian stopped the in and out canoe-like twirl of the oar and held it against his waist like a high wire artist might to balance on a high wire. The raft ran forward at speed to where I was stood on the diving board.

'What's happening?' I asked. 'Where are you going?' 'I've not come to rescue you,' he said breathing heavily. 'Right,' I said.

'I'm on my way to Blackberry Cove. Malks not turned up with Sea Spray.'

'It's back in action then?' Ian back stroked the paddles and expertly turned the raft to stand about ten feet away from the diving board.

'Yes, it was accessed at low tide and re-floated.

A spare engine was fitted,'

Elberry Cove was set to the western side of the main beach and offered protection from the south westerly blast, that whipped across Babbacombe Bay. In the evening when collecting deck chairs Sea Spray would be seen chugging out in front of a long line of pedalos on their way to the shelter of the small harbour with an inner dry dock.

'I'll join you,' I said and lowered myself into the space between raft and diving board. The sudden immersion in the sea took my breath away. I swam toward the stern of the raft and grabbed the back spreader, which served as a seat. Ian waited until I'd got a good hold before he paddled left and right, which caused the raft to zig-zag a bit from side to side through the sea. I lowered my head and pumped my legs as you would in a forward crawl.

'No need for that,' said Ian. 'Just hang on I'll provide the propulsion.' We were able to talk. There was hardly a breath of wind. Ian must have launched the raft shortly after I reached the diving board. He called back to me when the paddle moved back on either side for the next dip into the water.

'Malk's usually on the landing stage before the ferry arrives. They are starting a queue to use the pedalos early, with the weather being fine. He's probably overslept.' I'd seen Malk in the Cliff Side on occasions. Cliff Side was above the large beach hut he lived in during the summer season. We approached the harbour wall. The tide was, retreating. That fine emerald sea weed, which lives near the water edge was visible on the lower walls of the small harbour. A few dinghies and yachts with drop keels were moored in the harbour plus one or two cabined open motor boats. Ian expertly weaved through these. I admit to re-imagining the raft to be a canoe like in the Cockleshell

Heroes. A recent book I'd read about the Second World War and a daring attack on German shipping by a British commando force with canoes and limpet mines. The raft stood in for the cockleshell. The twin hulled raft was helped on to the slipway by a strong wave. Ian jumped ashore and grabbed the seat to haul it up the slipway. I swam around the back until I could walk on to the slipway, and assist in dragging the raft ashore.

'Just a little way up clear of the water,' said Ian. 'The tide's falling quite fast. It should be safe.'

I'd never been to Blackberry Cove, although it was visible from the windows facing the beach from the Cliff Side Hotel and pub. This beach was mainly sandy, but scattered with red sandstone rocks, now weathered by the, sea, and encrusted with weed and barnacles, but originally attached to the cliff

above. Set back under the cliff was a car park and a few numbered fishing boats hauled to the top of the beach. Lobster
pots and nets hung from the masts. A padlocked wire netted
enclosure next to the car park contained fishing equipment.

About twenty beach huts painted shocking pink, yellow
blue and green stood on a concrete path overlooking the car
park. A red earthen path to the right of the car park led to a
large hut with windows at the front. I followed Ian.

'That's Malk's summer residence,' he said pointing to the
hut above the beach.

'Hold on,' I said. – The stones on the path were slowing
my pace. I stepped gingerly on the pathway with Ian striding
ahead. Above the wooden veranda chiseled into a name
plaque was the name "Tranquil Harbour" in white against a
black background. Ian arrived at the wooden veranda first and
knocked on the door. Malk's window-fronted beach home
was painted white with blue window ledges. Ian waited a
moment then knocked again—then once more.

'That's strange.'

'Wait here,' he said. 'He may not hear if he's out the back.'
Ian opened the gate leading to a path down the side. I heard
his trainers scuff the sand blown from the beach on to Malks
Garden slabs. Moments later he ran back.

'Malk's lying on his floor in the kitchen – grab hold of this
bench Phil.'

'What are you going to do?' I asked.

'Bang the door open what do you think?' I didn't argue.
I did as I was asked and grabbed hold of the two-seat bench
made from cherry branches lashed together with what looked
like planking from the ferry launching platform. With, Ian, at
the other end I helped to man handle it around to the back
door. We used it like a battering ram to break the lock.

The door frame partly splintered as the bench smashed
into the door by the lock on our second attempt. We simultaneously let go of the bench once the door broke open.

Chapter 38

IAN AT THE FRONT was first in.

'Has he fainted,' I asked. The kind of hopeful remark you make, not wanting to assume the worst. He was lying on his front head towards a door that I imagined led into the living area and bedroom. Ian knelt and reached out with his hand to feel Malk's neck. I suppose this was instinctive for someone with first aid training who wanted to see if there was a pulse in the carotid artery) He was in jeans and tee shirt, but the mahogany burnished skin remained dark from weeks spent on the beach

'He's stone cold – he's been lying here for some time.' The light from the open door picked out the body, but left shadows either side. Ian was still knelt next to Malk, but he turned towards me. I must have looked startled, but we were both shocked.

'Do you think it's a heart attack?' I said. I then considered this as the possible cause of death. There was no evidence of a break in. The body was lying at an angle and we were both knelt on the same side. It was only when I stood up and Ian reached for his mobile that I noted that the blue carpet near to the sink was stained red.

'Look, that's blood. Isn't it?' Ian turned, raised his eyebrows, but attended to the voice on his phone. For some reason I walked across and opened the door leading into the living space. The body of Ambrose was sprawled across the arm chair faced towards me. I shall never forget the staring eyes and the way his right hand clutched the knife in a failed attempt probably to remove it. There was blood across the table, chairs, and carpet. He must have staggered about before collapsing in the arm chair.

'Ian,' I called out loudly to make sure he heard. 'Come and look at this.' He entered with the phone to his ear.

'Jesus,' he said, 'there's a body in the lounge, as well. He's been stabbed.'

'No, I'm not making it up. My name's Ian Duncan. I am a beach attendant.'

'She wants your name and address as well.' After I'd answered various questions, I handed the phone back to Ian. 'What a performance.' We didn't realize how bizarre and unlikely the situation must have appeared to the recipient of the call. That it could've been considered a hoax.

'Can't touch anything,' I said. 'It's a crime scene.' Ian pocketed his phone.

'Have to wait for Inspector Wexford,' he said. It was a trite comment, but it relieved the tension and horror of what we'd stumbled on. We stood in the doorway. I noticed Ambrose's wrist hanging over the chair the Rolex clearly visible. I remembered him boasting at how he acquired it and now it was really of little consequence. On turning towards the kitchen, where Malk lay – twin barrels of a shotgun, previously unnoticed were peeping out from behind the opened door. I retched, involuntarily, but nothing came up. Ian was behind me and I pointed at the gun.

'Shit,' he said. 'You don't think the contents of that's inside Malk.

Ian found the words that explained why I retched uncontrollably. He'd noticed me do this.

'You all – right?'

'Yes,' I said. 'Well not really – I wasn't expecting anything like this.'

'Me neither. There's a shower room and bedroom on the other side of the far door.' We both looked at each other.

'You don't think there could be another body in there?' 'Or two,' I said. The gallows humour was a way of relieving the shock and horror of what we'd both witnessed. We both noticed the blue flashing light of the police car winding down the beach road. The clock above the sink read five to nine.

169

'Let's get out into the fresh air,' said Ian. He held his phone
and started to make another call.

'They'll have given up queuing for pedalos by now,' I said
once outside. A quite inconsequential and pointless thing to
say

'What are we going to tell the cops,' I asked Ian.

'Exactly why we're here and what we've found, but not
from here.

We'll meet them by the front.'

'The police can look in the other rooms,' I said, before I
caught Bill, the inspector's voice. He was on the end of Ian's
phone, which he's placed on speaker mode.

'You what? That means I'll have to be selling deck chair
ticket for the rest of the day. They'll want witness statements
and there'll be all manner of questions. That's the two of you
out of action.' The fact that two people were dead on the adjacent beach in a beach hut didn't seem to register as all that
serious for Bill in his Beach Inspector role. We were both
standing on the veranda when the police were walking up
the path. The man was tall, bespectacled with dark receding
hair. The woman with fair hair tied in a ponytail. They were
wearing short sleeve shirts, flak type body jackets and the
woman a fluorescent tabard. The man approached first.

'They'll be a re-naming this hut after this, I should think.'
He pointed to the name Tranquil Harbour above where we
were standing.

'You are –?' 'Ian Duncan.'

'I'm Philip Norton,' I said. 'We work as deck chair attendants at Babbacombe..'

'We broke in when we saw him on the floor.' said Ian'

'We thought perhaps he'd fainted, or had a heart attack,'
I said.

'Not through this door?' asked the woman, who moved
forward to try the front door.

'No, around the back,'

'Lead on MacDuff,' the man said. We'd pulled the back door closed. It swung open, but now only on one hinge. When Ian pushed it, he disturbed a swarm of flies that were feasting on the bloodied carpet.

'You haven't touched anything?' she asked. We'd both stood aside from the door.

'Nope,' said Ian— 'Oh, I touched his neck to see if he was alive.'

'I opened that door,' I said pointing to the now closed living room.

'Body on floor,' said the first one. Although he wasn't writing this down.

'We forced an entry with the bench.'

'Yes, I can see that all right,' said the constable. The bench now lay on its back by the door.

'We've come across from Babbacombe beach,' said Ian. We thought Mr Styles might have fainted, when we saw him on the floor. We came across to see if he'd overslept. Then broke in to see if he was all right.' Ian spoke in a staccato type fashion. 'Evidently that's not the case,' said the policeman, who was wiping sweat from his forehead with a tissue, after the climb up to the hut. Not from seeing the body.

'There's blood on the carpet and a shot gun behind the door,' I said, as if I was the only one to notice the flies, which were disturbed when the four of us entered.

'The other ones sat in the armchair, in the living room.' I left out telling them about the knife stuck into Ambrose. I must have retreated into some world where the police see dead bodies regularly? And, that a knife killing might be every day for them with no need to sensationalize about it.

'Won't be needing our investigation branch, by the sounds of things, with you two, the constable said, with an affirming look at the woman PC. It was a relaxed tone perhaps in a way necessary to lighten the enormity of the situation.

'I'll check the inside of the hut,' said the woman PC. We

171

were informed that there were two, bodies she said (matter of fact like).

'Two that we've seen' I said.

'Check the appliances Myrtle, while you're there. We don't want the place catching fire and burning the evidence. Step outside you two. Forensic will want everything left just as it is. There was a blue ambulance light flashing through the trees followed closely by a police Range Rover.

'Inspector Stevens has arrived,' said the copper to the ashen faced Myrtle when she stepped out into the sunlight from inspecting the bod

'He'll be the one wanting to talk to you two.' We accompanied them back to the veranda.

'That ambulance is going to have a long wait,' Myrtle said. 'What are your names?' asked Ian.

Chapter 39

A MIDDLE-AGED MAN IN a suit followed by a younger one in jeans and blazer arrived at the top of the path.

'Beat us to it Hill,' said the one I guessed was the plain clothes inspector.

'Just driving along the Downs when we got the call Inspector. Two dead bodies inside.' He jerked his thumb over his shoulder to indicate and also glanced at PC Jackson for affirmation – she being the one who went inside to look.

'No sign of a break in, initially, Inspector,' he continued.

'These gentleman came on the crime scene first.' Once again we gave our names. Ian explained how we came over from Babbacombe to see if Malk had overslept. I must have appeared to be a holidaymaker in my swimming shorts. Ian looked like the professional deck chair attendant in life jacket and khaki beach trousers.

'I will be wanting a written report from the both of you straightaway. How you came to be here, as you mentioned plus time of arrival and when you discovered the bodies. While it's still fresh in your minds.' Bill was proved right about how the police would require reports filling in.

'Constable you and PC Jackson can get that organized later.

There's an entrance around the back I take it constable?'

'Yes, inspector, it's just as we found it.

'I should very much hope so.' PC Hill led the detectives around to the back entrance, while PC Jackson remained with us.

'Should you two be at work?' she asked, after the others disappeared around the back.

'I was,' said Ian.

'I should've started at eight thirty,' I said.

'Don't worry, after you've filled in the witness statement,

you'll be able to return to Babbacombe. Myrtle Jackson said it as if perhaps we'd had enough excitement and would want to return to the more normal world of work. When she turned and spoke the ponytail kind of twitched to one side. The luminescent tabard made her trim figure appear larger. I noticed Ian looked interested. Perhaps he didn't harbour any reservations about the police and of course there was the uniform. That attraction a man can have for a uniformed woman or vice versa. But I was still feeling very upset about Meila's email and Myrtle didn't float my boat, anyhow.

'Follow me. We'll sit in the car, so as not to disturb anything around the incident site.' Ian looked happy about this suggestion.

'You're shivering,' said Myrtle. She produced one of those tin foil covers to wear, with a clip around the neck. I just started shivering involuntarily, but it wasn't from the cold I realize now. It was a kind of after-shock reaction.

'There my luv that'll help you warm up.' This amused Ian when, she said it. But embarrassed me no end.

A white minibus type vehicle drew up after PC Jackson opened the boot of the police car. We were handed clip boards, biros, and incident forms, while all manner of equipment was carried up the path from the minibus.

Visitors stopped to gawp. PC Jackson got out of the driving seat and moved them on, before another police car arrived and took on the job of telling both cars and pedestrians to keep on moving whether going to or from the beach.

'You may be required as court witnesses later,' she said. 'You said you didn't touch anything. Have you entered the living area?

'I only opened the living room door,' I said.' 'I'll make a note of that.'

'We just stood inside the kitchen,' said Ian.

'It was when I opened the living room door area, that I saw Ambrose.'

'Who is Ambrose?' she asked.

'I've never met him,' Ian quickly said.

'He's a pianist who works part-time at the hotels along the front of the Downs,' I replied. 'I met him in the café a fortnight ago. That's how I know, who he is.

He's not really an acquaintance. He goes into the Red and White café on the Downs for coffee.

'I only know Mr Styles from working on the beach.'

'That's how you came to be at Tranquil Harbour this morning? She was looking through and checking what we'd written in the incident reports. This took about ten minutes. 'You were swimming before you came across?' She turned to question me from the driver's seat.

'On the diving board. I was lay on it.'

'I picked Phil up,' said Ian. He hitched a lift on the back of the float,'

'You're a deck chair attendant, as well?' She already knew this.

'Yes, but not due to start work until eight -thirty.'

'You've missed that start time,' she said glancing at her watch. It's gone nine. She appeared satisfied with our accounts leading up to discovering the bodies.

'Sign and date at the end. The Inspector or sergeant from CID will likely want to see you later in proceedings. We'll go back up and see if you can return to Babbacombe. Are you warmer now?' she asked me. I quickly said "yes" and handed the foil cover back when we were out of the police car.

The Inspector, who wasn't named Wexford, but Stevens wanted verification from Bill Simpson as to who we said we were. Ian called him on his phone and Bill must have been as undemonstrative about the murders as he was with Ian when he spoke to the police Inspector. The inspector meanwhile was talking with a paramedic with the words Emergency Doctor on the back of his tabard.

'Your inspector appears quite keen to have you back. The

175

medic also tells me that shock may set in, but that both of you will benefit from returning to your normal life experience. That's if it's not coming across dead bodies on a regular basis. The Beach Inspector tells me there's a demand for rafts, now there are no pedalos, apparently. You came over on a raft I take it?' Ian's rolled up trousers splashed with salt water allowed for this bit of deduction, no doubt.

'We can go then?' said Ian.

'Yes, but I will need to call you in later. You have their names, addresses, phone numbers, email addresses etc.... PC Jackson.'

'Yes, inspector I've done all that.' PC Jackson smiled as if she expected a pat on the back.

'I'll be in touch. Meanwhile you can return to Babbacombe,' said Inspector Stevens.

We walked down the path. There was a tent set up half way down and a police woman with the word Forensics across her back was standing talking to a white suited person wearing blue gloves, white overalls, and a face mask. When we reached the slipway there was a fifteen-foot gap between the raft and the water's edge. We carried the raft by the handholds down to the water's edge.

'I'll push off,' I said to Ian.

'Jump on the back seat then, it'll be easier for me to paddle,' said Ian from the front.

I could see Bill was standing on the ferry jetty when we got closer to Babbacombe. Every raft bar the one we were on was out in the bay.

Chapter 40

'**Am I glad to** see you two,' said Bill. Rushed off my feet.' He hooked the raft alongside and then held it by the galvanized ring welded into the bow section. Somehow Bill seemed able to detach himself from the enormity of what happened. He was an ex Royal Marine, which may have accounted for his way of handling the news of the two deaths.

'We think Malk was shot. The other one knifed,' said Ian as he jumped from the raft, to the landing stage with the painter. 'Then it was breaking and entering.'

'No,' I said, as I followed Ian on to the landing stage. 'The doors were both locked.'

'Still could've been attempted theft. Styles was always saying that he didn't trust banks. Kept his takings in a safe under the floorboards.'

'He told you that?' questioned Ian. Bill's answer was interrupted.

'Is that raft free?' A tanned teenager plus girlfriend ran up the landing stage towards where we were standing.

'Yes, it is now. Got your ticket?' The youngster held out two yellow tickets, bought from Julie at the railway ticket office. Bill clipped the two together before he handed them back.

'Do you want another set of paddles?' he asked.

'I'm not paddling dressed like this,' the girl turned to her boyfriend.

She was wearing a white handkerchief sized bikini held together with flimsy looking white string. The bikini top appeared similarly tied at the back. Neither looked very water resistant. A design more suitable for sunbathing, than swimming. Perhaps the boyfriend's plan of action involved more than keeping her dry while she sat on the raft. The contrast between the horrific scene in the beach hut and what we now witnessed appeared as a welcome relief from those recent memories. For me at any rate.

'I'll sit at the back and you can paddle. You can be like the cab driver,' she said.

'More like rickshaw driver,' the boy replied. He stepped on to the raft and helped her on to the plinth seat at the back.

'Oh, the water's cold out here,' she said, when she sat down. Her legs dipped into the water almost to knee height. The rapidly kicked feet, probably more an attempt to get – than from the cold. Bill handed the paddle over.

'Thirty minutes and you'll hear this.' Bill turned the handle on the klaxon horn attached to the post nearby and a wailing sound like a banshee momentarily took over the near quiet – save for the lapped water alongside the jetty.

This interlude interrupted discussion about the fate of Ambrose and Malcolm Styles.

'Here Ian take these,' said Bill. He removed the attendant's pouch and ticket machine strapped across each shoulder.

'Looks like I'm taking over a dead man's shoes running the rafts for the day. All this mob are getting a deck chair free holiday right across the beach. And those up on the hard.' Bill waved his arm towards the concrete below the steps.

'They've mostly been ticketed,' Bill said. 'These want catching before they decide to leave, because of the heat.' Ian removed his life jacket and swapped it for the machine and pouch.

'We're two short today. Dan's phoned in. He came off his mountain bike last night, apparently and twisted his ankle. He's at A&E and says he'll be all right with a pair of crutches. Just wants a parrot and a pistol and he could pass for Long John Silver. I'll want you to do a tour of duty on the Downs Phil.' A themed Beach Boys jingle started on Bill's phone.

'Yes, Stella I know Dan's not turned in today. I'm sending a replacement Now.' He cut short the call.

'What it's to do with her I'll never know. She doesn't

bleeding own the Downs, although the way she talks you'd think she was the lady of the manor.' There was a Babbacombe Manor Hotel – somewhat more resplendent than Mrs Brown's Red and White Rose café. Ian was already taking deck chair payment and handing out tickets when I walked with Bill up to the beach inspector's office. This was situated next to the yacht club' premises, which was accessible from an outside wooden stairway. The ground floor housed sails and there was an area for yacht repairs. It was the police no entry sign at the foot of the stairway, which caught my attention. I glanced across to the car park and three police Range Rovers were parked in a row across. Bill noticed me looking.

'They arrived shortly after Ian rang. We're now their campaign investigation headquarters. I can tell them without an investigation what happened. Styles, owed money to Ambrose and wasn't going to pay and Ambrose threatened him with his shot gun he uses for rabbiting and Bob's your uncle they killed each other.'

'Why would Malk owe money to Ambrose?' I asked. Bill tapped his nose.

'You're not a local lad, are you? Ambrose has got them all on a leash. Even them up there.' He pointed to the yacht club premises.

'The police?'

'Maybe even some of them, but yacht club members short of the readies wouldn't be surprised. When you need cash in a hurry Ambrose's your man. You've heard of Wonga lending?'

'Yes,'

'Well, Ambrose got there way ahead of them with his lending method.

Mark my words Phil that'll be what's behind these two killings.' This threw new light on everything.

'Perhaps you should mention this to the police.' I said all innocent. PCs Hill and Jackson would likely see Bill as a good informer.

'Not likely. – Before you know it, they'll be saying I was involved. Once they decide that someone fits the frame with a motive, you're likely to be in the firing line.

'You have a motive?'

'Yes, they're a couple of grasping toads and I for one won't miss them.'

'That's not a motive.'

'Well, it might be seen as one. Here we haven't time to stand and chat.

'Get in that rail car and start selling tickets up there.' Bill pointed to the railings above on the Downs, where you could look down on the beach and the blue sea. The thought of getting away from the beach in the aftermath of what we'd just experienced would normally have been appealing, but I felt a jolt inside when I remembered that Pamela was no longer in my life. The message said she was leaving Sea View to help her mother. It was Wednesday. While I travelled up in the rail car, I'd already decided that the Sea View Hotel would be my destination venue for transferring notes to coins from the deck chair sales.

Chapter 41

MY APPEARANCE BY THE fountain, which led to the Downs didn't go unnoticed by deck chairs occupants. This included a party of four with their own fold-away chairs.

Near to the cliff a path weaved in front of a narrow strip of grass occupied by transient holidaymakers. They were most likely waiting for a bus into town or otherwise undecided about their future day – unsure about whether go to the beach or town. This happened when the weather looked unsettled. it was overcast and the beach as a venue could quickly lost its allure.

Such was the power of my presence that the dozen or so nearest occupants plus the folding chair party stood up like they'd been stung by bees and walked away. The regulars, who intended staying paid but the vacating of chairs carried on as I approached.

When I glanced back some of these empty chairs were taken by new arrivals. It was a warm July day and pleasant even without the full sun.

On the balcony I met up with Maria and Sally. Their chairs were turned inwards towards the sun, which would rise high enough to reach Babbacombe beach just after midday They didn't notice my arrival, eyes closed. It was still possible to catch a tan, with a brisk breeze even with the scudding clouds.

'Tickets please.' Maria shaded her eyes before she spoke.

'Where's Dan?'

'Came off his mountain bike. You've got me instead,' I said.

'Is he all, right?' Asked Sal after she removed her sunglasses. 'He's twisted his ankle, but he's coming to work tomorrow.'

'Poor thing,' said Sal, but didn't look that concerned. 'He'll be back tomorrow, with a twisted ankle?'

Maria asked. 'He's able to get about on crutches.' Dan might even increase his fan base, if it turned out to be a fracture with a plaster cast. He would be collecting signatures, I was thinking.

I needed to talk to Maria. I wanted to tell her about the horrific discovery we'd made in Malk's beach hut. Bill's explanation that Malk owed money to Ambrose was a plausible reason for their attacking and killing each other— perhaps – after Bill told me abo the role of Ambrose as a money lender. The knife in Ambrose's chest was Malk's knife.

I'd seen Malk unsheathe it and dive from the landing stage into a shoal of fish. After a minute or so he would surface with a silvery fish, skewered and thrashing on the knife. He perhaps first threatened Ambrose with the shot gun Ambrose then could've snatched it off him. Malk knifing Ambrose, while Ambrose emptied the two barrels into Malk. With locked doors, Ambrose couldn't get out and bled to death in the armchair. It all seemed plausible after Bill explained that Ambrose was a money lender. The result of a disagreement over debt owed by Malk to Ambrose. The possibility of drugs coming ashore in the cool boxes –something totally unconnected with these killings.

I felt Maria was the only person I could turn to and I wanted to talk with her on her own. I didn't want to talk about the horrific discoveries of the bodies of Ambrose and

Malk with Sally sat next to her and others nearby likely to earwig. I wasn't going to let that happen.

'Will you be here until one o'clock?' I asked Maria. 'Could be.'

I don't start serving at Cliff Side until one forty -five.

'If I take my break at one,' I said, 'can we meet at the Red and White Rose café?'

'Don't mind me,' said Sal, who mouthed the words, and looked down, in a dejected sort of way.

'You can come too,' I quickly added, although this defeated the object of the exercise.

'No, you can have Maria all, all, to yourself; I'm due back in half an hour.' Sal put her arm around Maria, made as if to kiss her on the cheek, smiled at me, then let her go free. There was nothing going on between us. Only the shared confidences about Alfie, and the need to find out more.

We'd become friends, that's Maria and me, after our meeting at the hospital. That was all. I felt that Maria was the person I wanted to talk to about the blood bath in Malk's beach hut. I looked at my watch. It was twelve thirty or thereabouts. Time to complete another circuit of the Downs before my break. Maria handed me a fifty pence piece in exchange for two tickets.

'See you at the Red and White then,' I said. Ian and my discovery of Malk and Ambrose in the beach home likely to appear in the weekly Babbacombe Express.

It would certainly be reported nationally, but that would likely follow on from a police press conference. They might not want news coverage today, while forensics were studying the crime scene, although I could imagine the headline— "Bodies discovered by beach attendants in beach home."

The half hour passed quickly with another circuit of the Downs. Maria and Sal were no longer on the balcony when I looked across and there were no new deck chair customers, the brisk breeze on top perhaps putting them off. I walked toward the Red and White Rose café, but the earlier experiences on Blackberry beach flooded back.

Psychologically the police getting the both of us back with our work colleagues was probably the right policy. PC Myrtle Jackson said that she expected we'd be given counselling later. Though I imagined that should happen straightaway.

Maria looked up – lips around a straw from the Pepsi bottle when I entered.

Brightness, of the sun, made those normally dark brown eyes look black, but she smiled.

I raised my hand and smiled back from just inside the open door. Maria was sat at a table away from the counter. 'I'll bring it to you luv,' said Mrs Brown. She'd noticed Maria's smile before I ordered a Coke.

'Don't usually have your break in here, but can see you've a good reason to now,' she said with a glance towards Maria. There were two couples sat near the window, but otherwise the café was empty. I decided not to say that Ambrose wouldn't be in today – nor ever again for that matter. Maria greeted me with,

'You're back at work, Phil, then?'

'You as well,' I replied. 'No after effects, then?'

'Only that I'll never be going in a boat again, unless I learn to swim.'

'You can do that now,' I said. I sat in the chair opposite. 'You're right next to the sea.'

'Ah, I was also in Galway Bay. But perhaps I'll have another go. You wanted to see me, Phil? About the cool boxes? And you'll still be delivering them. Tomorrow.'

'Yes, I hope so with Dan back. But there's something else. I don't know how to say this. I don't want to surprise or startle you.'

'It isn't about you and Pamela?' It could've been. A pain stabbed at my side, because it brought home how I felt. Maria perhaps could sense that things weren't going right for me. The bloodied bodies of Ambrose and Malk in the hut hadn't taken away my deep feeling of hurt from Meila's email. I certainly didn't arrange to meet Maria to talk about Pamela or my love for her. My reaction, I felt from the question, made me realize that this was what was uppermost in my mind, even after what Ian and I'd witnessed!

'No, everything's okay,' I said, with feigned indifference. It was evident that Maria knew Pamela. That my love for her and our relationship no longer a secret. But I was still trying to convince myself, that it could be Pamela, who wanted to cool things and that we would be back together. Once she'd helped her mother settle into the boutique. I moved my arms from across the table.

'Thanks, Mrs Brown,' I said, after she'd first brushed the table ostentatiously with a white cloth, half –filled a glass of frothing Coke and carefully placed the bottle at its side.

'Will that be all, sir?' Maria was amused that we were made a fuss of.

'Yes, thanks,' I smiled at Mrs Brown and her cabaret act of pretend deference. I'm not hungry Mrs Brown. It's too hot. 'Not like you to not want a slice of apple pie.' I wished she'd go away. I was thirsty, but not hungry and I wanted to talk to Maria. A couple entered and stood by the counter.

'Be right with you, sir. Trays can be taken out on the Downs with a small deposit, if you wish.' She hurried back to the counter to serve the new customers. More important, than entertaining the likes of me and Maria.

Chapter 42

'IF IT'S NOT ABOUT you and Pamela, what is it about?' Maria looked across at me and syphoned the remaining Pepsi, until the straw made that gurgling sound in the bottle.

'It's not good news. This morning I swam out to dive from the board before I started work.

'Anyway, while I was there Ian arrived paddling a raft. He was off to wake Malk.'

'Who's Malk?' I realized Maria would have no idea.

'He's the guy who owns the pedalos, rafts and the ferry or he was. His full name is Malcolm Styles.

'Was? How do you, mean was?'

'We broke into his beach home. There was no answer. We went around the back and he was lying face down on the kitchen carpet. Smashed open the door with a garden bench to get in. At first, I thought he'd collapsed with a heart attack.' Now Maria, was lean forward to listen more intently.

A customer walked by on her way to the back of the café. I lowered my voice.

'He was dead Maria. Ian couldn't find a pulse. His neck was cold. He'd been dead some time. I opened the door into the lounge and Ambrose was sprawled across an arm chair, blood smeared on his hands and the chair from a knife in his chest.'

'That's really gruesome.' Maria put her hand to her face and gasped out –

'I can't believe you're telling me this, Phil. Whoever would've wanted to kill them?'

'That's it. They may've argued and killed each other. That's according to the Beach Inspector. Ian called the police and we gave statements, like incident reports. The medic doctor, who arrived in the ambulance recommended we return to our jobs. I'm glad he did. It now seems like it just couldn't have happened. Specially in a holiday resort.

'It's horrific. Maria shook her head and shivered. Makes me shudder just thinking about it.'

'Anyway,' I continued, 'after filling the incident reports in we went back to Babbacombe beach on the raft.' Bill, the Beach Inspector just sort of shrugged his shoulders, when we arrived back. He said that Malk owed money to Ambrose. He reckoned they killed each other.

'Yes, you said, but how could he possibly know that?" asked Maria.

'Did you know Ambrose Maria?'

'Yes, he's the one that sings and plays the piano. He's at the Cliff Side on a Friday. Sal calls him Mr Slime Ball. I didn't know he was into lending money.'

'Neither did I. There was a shot gun, broken open behind the door. It looked like the contents were inside Malk, judging by the blood on the carpet. Both the front and back door were locked. When I think about it Bill could be right. With the doors locked, who else would have keys?'

'Unless the killer locked the doors on the way out,' said Maria. I'd not thought of that.

'Bill knows them better than me. I just had Ambrose down for a slime ball as Sal said, who fleeced lonely women on holiday. Bill never seemed that concerned only that there were no pedalos and that he was forced to stand in for Malk's not being there and hire out rafts.'

'You never know it may just be a way of dealing with it for him,' said Maria.

There was a momentary silence. Both of us, at the same time struck by the horror of what had happened.

'The police phoned the Beach Inspector's office to find out if we were telling the truth about who we said we were. After describing how we got in to the hut and then filled in forms we were allowed to return to Babbacombe and here I am back on the Downs, standing in for Dan much the same as usual.

'I don't think I could return to work like that – who else have you told?'

'No one – that's why I wanted to meet you here. It's not something I want to share with just anyone.

'You don't think it's drug related? I mean,' said Maria, 'I mean connected with the cool boxes. That's if drugs are really concealed inside them?'

'Why should these killings be linked?' It's a different beach and –

– I stopped. A group of school girls deposited themselves on a table nearby, but they were oblivious to us. In fact, their cries of 'let me see,' while looking at I-phone pictures took attention away from us and the possibility of anyone over-hearing.

'And, anyway, the ferry brings in all sorts,' I continued. Not only cool boxes, but it supplies the beach café with papers, magazines, tins of beans all sorts.

There's no evidence that the ferry owner or anyone else would know about a shipment of drugs, if their hidden away inside the boxes.

'I can't really stay much longer Phil. Perhaps I should say thanks for sharing this with me—but it's so terrible that the two of them have probably killed each other – over money. 'Are you sure you're all, right? I valued Maria's concern. These recent events were taking my mind off the break with Pamela. Even though the sight of the two dead bodies scared the wits out of me

'Course I am.' I said, with more confidence than I felt.

Maria changed the subject.

'What should we do if you discover drugs in the cool boxes tomorrow?'

'I've thought about that. I overheard a conversation between John Langridge, the owner and, a guest when I first went to Sea View. The guest said he was a Chief Inspector with CID. He told John Langridge this while I was by the reception, but it was to be kept secret.

'Not very secret if you overheard. 'They weren't to know I was listening.' 'And this was when you met Pamela?'

'Yes, but that hasn't got anything to do with it.' Maria lifted her eyebrows, smiled, and moved her head from side to side disbelievingly.

'I was just getting the invoice stamped—doing my job,' I pleaded.

Maria placed, elbows on table, hands on cheeks and said, 'Right, okay, if you say so.'

'He wanted the owner to call him Jim Watson, not Chief Inspector and that he was acting incognito as the area manager for Harper and Smith.

'Don't they make wafers and cornets for ice cream? Their names all around the top of the cone.'

'Yes, it must've been cleared with the company for the Chief Inspector to go incognito as one of their area managers. It's making more sense now.

Maybe he knows about the drugs going to Sea View and is keeping tabs on the hotel to find out who's behind it. I was getting the invoice stamped by Pamela. They were standing apart from the reception desk.

'Pamela's left the hotel completely,' said Maria. 'You do know that?'

'Yep, 'I tried my best to look indifferent, but the look in Maria's eyes said that didn't work.

'I'll be up here tomorrow with the cool boxes. I'll be able to get into the secret compartments. The ones Alfie found.

'You'll let me know if you find anything.

'What's your mobile number?

'Maria rummaged in her hand bag and produced her mobile.

'I've got my number on the saved list. Can never remember it,' she said.

'0778467992,' she read out. I punched the number into my

number memory contacts just above Pamela's. I was tempted to call Pamela back, but I admit feared rejection. I'd wait a few more days and casually mention about meeting for a coffee, as she suggested. That was then the plan.

Chapter 43

WE BOTH LEFT THE table. Maria was due back at the Cliff Side and I decided to visit Sea View to get some coins. I forgot to ask Mrs Brown if she had any pounds or fifty pence pieces. When I arrived at the hotel there was this banner, which said – H & S Conference Venue outside the front window of the breakfast room attached to folded table umbrellas. It was about ten feet long and it flapped in the breeze, which made the metal table bases lift and fall. A strong wind could upend them. There were signs and placards in the entrance area. Another banner suspended over the reception, stated.

CONFERENCE MEMBERS FOR S&H
FIRST SIGN IN AT
RECEPTION, PLEASE

There was no one at reception. Then Olga stood up from underneath holding a lap top.

'Phil, you are just in time.' She placed the lap top on the desk and spun it around.

'I'm supposed to find out the next weeks guest appointments on here and print it out – next week's guest list for Mr Langridge.' The printer was attached to the lap top. I noted the make of the printer and type. It was different from the one on the screen.

'You know how to make it print?' I adjusted the setting on the printer.

'How many copies Olga?'

'Five. Mr Langridge wants five.' I set it for five and after these were printed out, I asked Olga about the Conference.

'It was on Monday.'

'Why are the banners not down?

'Mr Langridge say to leave them until end of week. It

impresses the guests that there is a conference here. They might want to have one, as well.'

'Where was it?' I asked.

'Upstairs in Library room. Mr Langridge says it was very hush hush. Not quiet where no one talks, but secret.' I bet, I thought, if there was a convening of CID under the guise of a business meeting. I remembered chatting with a civil servant, who said police never advertised a meeting where high-ranking police officers were in attendance.

They would disguise the meeting. In one case, she said, they held it in a marquee where a flower judging competition was in progress. They were wearing judges' badges, but none of them knew much about flowers. This purported luxury cake company meet up at Sea View appeared like a similar diversion. To not only fool the public, but perhaps also the organized criminal fraternity.

Chapter 44

MARIA MESSAGED ME AT eight o'clock, on my way to the beach that Friday

"Hi Phil," it said and "Don't forget to let me know what you find in the cool boxes today, Lots of Love, Maria." I liked the way she ended the message and that she got back so soon. I'd intended to message, but she was the one who really wanted to know about whether it was true about drugs coming ashore. At this point I was helping out. I really didn't know what to expect. Maybe the drug smuggling was at an end. I tried to stop myself saying that my relationship with Pamela could be over. She, never said it was over. It was because something had happened. Something she could not tell me about now. I persuaded myself that when we met for coffee we could pick up from where we left off. That we were passing through that high intensity phase to a more companionable acceptance. That she was putting family first. A quite natural thing for a daughter to do. That this was a breathing space for the both of us. That, that, that— excuses really.

I was also trying to put yesterday's experience of seeing two dead bodies out of my mind. When something horrific happens, you can resort to returning to your everyday life to get over it. That was where I was then—another that!

I opened my locker and put the jacket I was wearing over my beach uniform inside.

There was this scuffed leather bag in the corner of the beach inspector's office. I looked inside, out of curiosity when I first started on the beach expecting to find bats, stumps, pads, and bails, but was surprised to find a croquet set. Apart from the hoops, ball, and long handled mallets there was I remembered in the equipment a small wooden mallet ideal for tapping the base of a cool box to slid it open. I scrabbled in the bag, found it, and placed it in a plastic carrier together with a can of Coke for later. I later loaded the cool boxes from the ferry and steered from the beach to opposite the ticket office. Julie waved and I waved back but the rail car arrived and I didn't stop to chat. Apart from the guard on the way up from the beach, there was no one else, which was good.

At the top the sign indicating the beach path was closed meant no one would bother to walk around the corner. I swung the handle across and went around that corner leading to the now closed entrance. A zinging from the lines meant the rail car was on it return to the beach. The path was now quite overgrown, which helped in concealing the truck from view.

I jerked the steering handle upwards, which braked the truck where it was. I unclipped the criss-crossed securing straps and lifted a cool box on to the path. I turned it on its side and with the mallet tapped the base, which started to slide apart from the main body of the box. The inner part held a steel tray, but it was empty. The base slid back into its snug position, and I removed another box. The same result again. Just the shiny inner metal tray. Time was moving on. I chose a box from the next row along.

This time on removing the base a flattened heavy duty clear polythene bag filled with white powder revealed itself. I ran my finger along the tube and licked it. There was a bitter taste. A shiver went through me. It was the large amount of the powder and the realization that if it was cocaine – it had a street value of many thousands of pounds. It would need close inspection by experts. I picked up the base and on the side was a white star. That most probably was an indicator to reveal the presence of drugs. The star appeared to have no purpose and was indiscreet blending in with the white of the polystyrene outer cover. The other two that I'd opened lacked this marking. I rapidly unstacked a few more and two others were marked with a white star.

The rail stopped its zinging, which meant the return rail

car was near to the top and easing its way into the buffers. I rapidly re-stacked the boxes, threw the straps over the top and released the brake. The straps could be adjusted in place away from the railway.

The guard might question why I was still near to the railway after being transported to the top by the other car.

The beach road curved around to meet the main busy road along the Downs. I stopped the other side of the fountain in the shadow of the angel's verdigris green wings hidden from the railway. I re-secured the straps before continuing to Sea View.

'Where've you been – Speedy Gonzales,' said Joe, is doing his nut.' I'd thought of an answer.

'The rail cars are busy. I had to wait until the queue went down Joe.'

'Okay. Okay, you are here now.'

To make up for lost time I both unload the full boxes and helped Joe load the empties on to the truck into from outside refrigerated pantry. Purposely I stacked the ones with the white star near to the door. I went through the kitchen to get the invoice stamped as delivered. Olga looked flustered, but smiled when she saw me.

'Olga,' I said. Is Mr Watson in the hotel?' 'Yes, he is having breakfast. Why you ask?'

'I need to talk with him. Has he been long in the breakfast room?'

'He always finished by nine. It is nearly nine now,' She turned to look at the clock on the wall above the reception.

'While Olga ratcheted the hotel received goods stamp on to the invoice. I asked,

'How's it going with your new work as replacement receptionist Olga?'

'Not good, but I manage' I wanted to find time before Mr Watson finished his breakfast.

'I've some time to spare. Is there anything I can help you with?'

195

Olga's anxious look disappeared and produced the receptionist's lap top from the shelf beneath the desk.

'Yes, there are one or two things. You are very kind Phil. I so wish Pamela was still here.' I almost said, "me to," but stopped myself.

Chapter 45

I NEEDED A REASON to stay by the reception. Long enough for Mr James Watson, the masquerading area biscuit manager for Harper and Smith's to finish his breakfast. I managed to access a folder about future bookings. This excited Olga.

'Look it is a coach party from Poland. I recognize the name on the coach. It is for twenty nine September. It will be cheap stay then and I will be able to speak to them in my own language. That is good,' she said.

'Do you still see Pamela, Phillip now she is left hotel? I miss her very much.'

'You're not the only one,' I replied, which sort of answered the question, but not by saying Pamela had broken off from seeing me. The second of the double doors was pushed open by John Langridge, with a flourish that implied he was relieved that breakfasts were coming to an end. Perhaps, even an encouragement for guests to leave the breakfast area.

He walked across to the reception. I picked up the stamped invoice and made as if it had just been stamped and needed checking.

'Everything all right Olga,' he said, after he lifted the flap, which allowed access to the reception desk behind.

'Yes, it is now Mr Langridge,' she smiled at me, but I'd spotted Mr Watson striding out of the breakfast room making for the stairway. I walked across to intercept him as he placed a foot on the stairs. I was direct.

'Mr Watson you are CID. I mean you're not really an area manager for S&H, are you?' I said in a quiet voice, but I spoke directly to him. He looked startled and surprised at my question.

'How did you know? It looks like my covers blown,' he said.

'It's top secret my CID role. Have you something to tell

me?' He looked at his watch and back at me. I was in no hurry, to go anywhere, but he appeared to be. I decided to come straight out about what I'd found hidden in the cool boxes.

'It's Phil, isn't it?' he said. There was no reason why he should have known my name, but John Langridge had a mouth like a barn door, always gossiping to guests.

'Yes, Chief Inspector. The cool boxes, the ones I bring from the beach to the hotel I believe contain drugs. They're hidden in trays in the bottom section, but only in those which have a white star fixed to the box. That's as far as I can tell. I mean there's this fine white powder with a bitter taste. The powders in heavy duty polythene bags.

'Really?' He looked surprised. 'This seems like the break-through we've been looking for.'

You brought these boxes in today?'

'Yes – I've got the invoice for them being delivered.' I undid the pocket button of my shirt and took out the invoice as evidence.

'John, John,' he called and once his attention was attracted, he imperiously raised a hand and waved for the hotel manager to break off from what he was doing pronto and come over. The manager looked anxiously across, and rushed to open the reception flap, almost trapping his coat, as it fell, in the haste. 'The fridge freezer where the cool boxes are stored can you show me where that is?'

'Of course, of course Jim. Not a problem follow me.' The Chief Inspector signaled for me to accompany the two of them. We went through the baize door, which led to the kitchen.

'Mr Langridge,' called out Carlos. 'Can I be of help, por favor?' He held a ladle, which he'd already raised to his mouth for a tasting, but lowered it to speak.

'I need to visit the cold room Carlos, if that's all right. Check on the latest order.'

'But, of course, you help yourself. We have busy week end

for cream teas. There are two coach parties. I hope we now have plenty.' He turned back to the task in hand. I followed the other two out to the yard and across to the cold room first grabbing the mallet from the carrier bag around the drive handle of the truck. The cool boxes were stacked next to crates of fresh vegetables and boxes of Golden Delicious apples.

'Ah you came prepared to open the boxes. May I ask how did you know about this? You said that it is the ones with the white star on the outside, said the Chief Inspector.

'It was Maria, the step sister of the previous deck chair attendant.'

'Such a shame, that he died suddenly,' said John Langridge. But he'd had a good life. We all die sometime.' I upended the first box in the stack, which was white starred

'Yes, yes, but what did she know that led to suspecting there were drugs?' asked the Chief Inspector.

'There was a letter to Maria inside his pocket book, which he never sent. It was with his belongings held by the local police. It said that there was a white powder that tasted sharp in the base of a cool box. One must have split open.'

'And they never spotted this letter. It's good that you two didn't just go to the local police force. Now I can do a thorough investigation.

I tapped the base of the cool box, which slid away to reveal the sachet of white powder.

'Well done for making that discovery,' said the Chief Inspector. He knelt, and picked the sachet out of the indented space.

'This isn't part of your delivery is it, John?

'No Jim, I mean Chief Inspector. I'm totally astonished about this. I never knew there were even concealed compartments in the cool boxes. You know I give every assistance I can to yourself and your team. It's frightening to believe that Sea View is receiving this stuff under our very noses.' The Chief Inspector sniffed the package before placing it back in the space it came from. I sensed that he was very familiar with the constituency and possibly even the smell of cocaine in this refined state.

'I'll need forensics to have tests completed, but this could be a breakthrough. Just what I've been looking for John.'

'I expect there'll be a reward for Phillip, don't you think Jim?'

'Indubitably,' said the inspector as he got to his feet. He went outside, presumably to ensure he got a good mobile phone signal. Babbacombe was in the back and beyond for mobile signals. John Langridge and I followed him outside.

'Yes, Baxter get the team on to it pronto. Yes, forensics will need to do tests on site. A stash has been intercepted at Sea View. You'll need to alert the coastguard, customs, and harbour master. It may well be from one of the cruise ships –

Over here at the Sea View Baxter!'

'You'd best return to duties. We'll take it from here,' he said. 'Oh, before you leave Phil do you have a contact number for Maria?' Is she staying locally? – I take it you two keep in touch.'

'Yes, Chief Inspector, she works at the Cliff Side. I accessed Maria's number and handed my phone over for him to record it.

'What about the truck?' I said. 'Shall I take it with me?' He handed my phone back before answering.

'No leave it for now. My team will need to inspect it. I'll be in touch. Invaluable bit of information.' He shook my hand and shortly afterwards I left the hotel for the beach. I remembered to phone Maria.

'It was drugs or seems to be Maria. Hidden in sachets in a lower shelf. I've had to leave the truck at the hotel. There's a team of police and other experts been called in to inspect the drugs. I was walking back to catch the rail carriage down to Babbacombe beach.

'Alfie was right then,' said Maria, and if I hadn't found that letter nothing would be done about the drugs being smuggled in.

'I hope it's all right Maria the Chief Inspector would like to get in touch. He asked for your mobile number and where you worked.

'Not sure about giving me mobile number out Phil, but it is the police. They could find out anyway, I suppose. By the way I've just met Pamela in Paignton, she would like to meet you for a coffee Phil.'

'Really,' I said. Things were looking up.

'She knows about your terrible experience—finding the bodies in the beach House. She wants to meet up with you as soon as possible.'

'Really,' I said again.

'Don't keep saying really. There's a quayside café called Seaside Rendezvous. It's opposite Pamela's mother's boutique.'

'Where's that?'

'Do you know the Paignton Quayside shopping precinct?'

'Yes – by the harbour where the ferry lands from Babbacombe.'

'The café is opposite to Rita's Boutique in the precinct.

I' did the right thing, Phil?' said Maria

'What was that, Maria?' We lost the signal. I missed what Maria said

'I said you'd meet her after work at five thirty tomorrow.

At the café. I did the right thing saying that?'

'Yes, Maria. I mean I've been meaning to catch up with Pamela.'—

I was dying to see her again, but I didn't tell Maria.

'She seems keen to see you Phil. I thought you were going out anyway.' I' d kind of lost contact with the real everyday world at the mention of Pamela, but I wasn't going to say that it was Pamela who ended the relationship.

'If she doesn't hear from you Pamela said she'll expect to see you at five thirty, at the café.

'Thanks Maria, got to go.' *I won't be messaging was the first thought to cross my mind. I would be at the Rendezvous Cafe by five thirty tomorrow.*

Chapter 46

THE FIGURE ON THE Norton Dominator, which drew up on the tarmacked quay, was indiscriminate. Indiscriminate in that the period helmet, bike and leathers could have in fact belonged to any number of bikers in Paignton, that Friday. When the tide fell back, a sandy stretch of beach became home to an army of vintage motor cycles. The esplanade nearby had scattered along its front with banners advertising the rally for now much treasured British bikes. Tomorrow, Friday was trophy day. The rider, dismounted near to the railings and kicked the stand out. He lowered on to the tarmac, and stood up, removed his gloves, and placed them on the pillion. He released clips from the white box on the back and removed a plastic encased chain and padlock, which he slipped through the front fork and around the nearby lower railing, clicking the open padlock shut. He re-aligned the numbers on the dial of the padlock. He kept his helmet and leathers on picked up the gloves and walked around the stretch of concrete, above the small harbour to a back entrance used by the shops for deliveries. He opened the blue paneled wooden door, studded at the top with spikes and barbed wire, with a long silver key taken from the top pocket of his leathers. The perforated metal stairs, which led to the top floor of Rita's flat, clanged each time his boots tapped on them. A light appeared in the wire-strengthened glass in the door above before he arrived at the railed platform outside. The door had been left open off the latch. The visitor entered

'John what the hell are you doing here? This isn't in the script.'

Alex was standing outside a half-opened door, which led into the main living room of the flat. He'd just returned from a two-day visit to London.

'Maybe not, but you've got to get away Alex. Pedro's taken out two local dealers. One that Malcolm Styles. There was a disagreement over the street price.

They wanted to increase prices and still pay Pedro the same as before. He went along with it, spiked their drinks near to closing and would you believe it used the ferry owners' knife to finish them both off.'

'Where are the bodies?' asked Alex. 'Not still at the Blue Comet?'

'No, we loaded them into the Sea View minibus and took them to Styles' beach home. We made it look as if there'd been a dispute and left a shot gun nearby and put one with a knife in his chest in the armchair. Locked the back door on the way out. 'They'll realize that the deaths didn't occur in the hut, surely,' said Alex.

'Not straightaway. Already there's a story going around that they probably rowed over money. We never should've recruited that pianist as a dealer Alex he was a loan shark. The Beach Inspector has already said he believes they argued over money and this resulted in them killing each other.

'It gives us breathing space, if the filth goes down that track first,' said Alex.

'Pedro's booked on a flight back to Lima. He'll be safe once he gets there,' said John Langridge. The enactment of John Langridge as hotel manager and Alex pretending to be a Chief Inspector for the benefit of deceiving Phil, no longer operative, now that they were both away from the Sea View Hotel.

He brushed his boots on the mat, while unstrapping the crash hat. The murders both spoken about as if they were regular hiccoughs that were not of much consequence.

'Rita and Pamela here?'

'Yes John.' Rita replied listening to the conversation from the next room. Pamela until then was in the kitchen, but returned to the lounge with a coffee.

'Who's that mother?'

'A business partner of your father's, that is all,' replied Rita.

'The games up for getting consignments into the hotel, John,' said Alex. Now that the beach attendants rumbled there're secret compartments. Our plan to ensure the attendant delivering the cool boxes believes that I'm kosher CID and informs me of possible smuggling directly has played out. Fortune favours the brave John. That was the last ferry to shore consignment. Come on in.'

'Which chair attendant is that asked Pamela,' before she turned towards the door and recognized her former boss, John Langridge.

'Hello Pamela.

'I don't get this. How do you three know each other.'

'It's all right Pammie John is partner with your father. It is better you did not know this.'

'We went to RADA together,' said Alex. John here belonged to the Royal Shakespeare Company for a while. John Langridge placed gloves and crash hat on a straight-backed chair by the door, knelt and unzipped his boots.

'Do not bother to remove it is not best carpet,' said Rita.

By which time he was stepping out of his boots.

'Okay, okay. It is all right sit where you like,' continued Rita.

'I got some minor roles,' said John, who sat in the chair opposite to where Pamela.

'You do yourself down John. You played Claudius in that play,' said Alex, who joined his wife on the sofa.

'I played police roles Pamela mainly for television plays before the allure of serious real-life role playing came along. Before I met your mother.'

'You do not say Alex that you play policeman roles. You say to me that you were lead actor in plays, like film star, like Gregory Peck not just policeman,' said Rita

'I played the lead role in theatre productions as well,' said

Alex aiming to recover status in the eyes of Rita. He continued explaining.

'The business has shares in the hotel and what better person to run it than John master actor. Man of disguise.'

'You still haven't answered my question, father,' Pamela interrupted.

'It's okay Pamela,' said her mother. 'It is the one you are no longer seeing.'

'Why is that all right? And what is this about being informed of possible drug smuggling. The previous attendant died of a heart attack on the beach. Didn't he? – That's what you said. It's all lies this set up with me getting a receptionist's job.

'No that is all true, Pamela. There was a vacancy for a receptionist,' said Rita

'A vacancy in a hotel run by you two.'

'No Pamela,' said her father. 'John runs the hotel for us and there was a genuine vacancy.'

'But, that Alfie–?'

'The deck chair attendant – he didn't die of a heart attack as everyone believed,' said her father. He found out about the sachets hidden in the cool boxes. The cruise ships started arriving in February. It was May, when he came to me in the hotel, he believed me to be CID, and the season lay ahead. The last consignment for the month was that week.

A week later and there would've been nothing hidden in the boxes. As it was only five boxes contained a pay load consignment.

'You told me this time there were no more. That's why you wanted me to leave and help mother with the boutique.'

'Yes, but there was a change of plan.'

'The other attendant was killed on your instructions though.

How was he killed,' asked Pamela.

'He was old,' said John and he was diagnosed as having had

a heart attack. It was not a problem until that Maria turned up and started asking questions at Sea View about whether anyone knew her step brother.

'How did he die then?' continued Pamela, like a terrier gripping a rat and not willing to let go.

'He didn't have a heart attack, did he?' said Pamela. 'It was all a cover up, because he was killed. How did you kill him?'

'Yes, unfortunately there was really no other choice,' said John Langridge. I sent Pedro from the Blue Comet. He was able to draw him away from everyone else on the beach by taking a deck chair behind boulders on the beach. After he bought a ticket, he asked the time and then grabbed his wrist pulled him face down and injected Diphenhydramine into his ear. The compound breaks down quickly within the body. It's the fifth time he's used this method.

It was all working well until this Maria turned up and now Pedro's had another killing session.' Pamela, said nothing, but felt vindicated by the feeling, that she had about Pedro.

'You're not implicated Alex. You were in London, I will say when they start making enquiries, which they're sure to do. You don't want to be here. I can give a witness statement that I believed you were CID. I'm good at playing the bumbling hotel manager. The deck chair attendant, believed you were CID, as intended, but you sure as hell need to get away Alex.'

'You will accompany me, Pamela. We will leave for Spain,' Alex said.

Chapter 47

THERE WAS THE CLATTER of plates cups and cutlery from the kitchen behind the counter space, but a stillness in the café. I was sat inside and unaware of Pamela's arrival until she called my name.

'Phill-ip. Why are you sitting indoors. It's a nice summer evening.'

'Hi, I said. Pamela, silhouetted in the doorway called across as she entered. She removed bands around a ponytail and black hair cascaded on to her shoulders.

The belt between her tee shirt and jeans was green with glass studs. This style of dress adopted, no doubt, for working in the boutique.

'The shop's closed now. I've come straight over. It's all right I'll buy myself a drink,' she said before I'd time to ask.

'I will have a Pepsi with ice and lemon,' she said to the barista.

'One Pepsi with ice and lemon it is, then.' I picked up my coffee and walked across.

'Are you all right Phill-ip? I miss you so much she said. The tiles caused the rubber on her trainers to squeak as she kissed my cheek on tiptoe before removing change from hipster jeans pocket to pay. A feeling of peace and harmony with the world returned. We walked outside.

'Marie passed on my message. I've wanted to contact you before Phill-ip, but there has been no time.' Pamela walked over to the farthermost table and chairs. There was no one nearby. We sat down opposite each other.

'I've missed you, Meila,' I said in understatement.

'That is sweet of you,' she said. I noticed a change. That immediate frisson reduced. We were after all just meeting for coffee.

'I felt how terrible it was, Phil-ip after the boat sank and

208

you'd only just gone back to work and you found those two dead bodies. It was on, the front page of the local paper and on the television news. I heard about it first from Maria, when she visited the boutique Meila looked away before continuing and then stretched her hand across the table, which I took hold of momentarily.

'It's so quiet here,' she said. There was a smile for me.

'I like you so very much Phill-ip – it must have been terrible for you just recently.'

'Do you want to meet again. I mean go out?' I was quick to pursue the possibility of this.

'I would like too very much.' Her brown eyes did look hurt almost like those of a wounded animal, but it was as if decisions were not of her making.

That a more powerful force or forces controlled her life at that point. I was trying to think then how the discovery of Ambrose and the ferry owner could have affected our relationship, but it wasn't just that. Meila ran her hand further along the table towards me. I held those slender fingers. She smiled and then withdrew again to pick up the glass of Pepsi. Her eyes darted from side to side, as if looking to see if anyone else was nearby. The quayside was deserted save for a gull several tables away aggressively pecking a discarded ice cream cone.

'I have to leave with my father. We are going to Spain,' she said emphatically. Her eyes pleaded for me not to ask more, but just accept what she told me.

'I cannot give all the reasons, Phill-ip, just now. It is about the family business and needs to be kept a secret. You do understand Phill-ip—that is if you love me?

'Of course, I do. You know I do Meila. Does your father live here?' I asked. I could see curtains in the rooms above the boutique.

'That – is the boutique?' I enquired pointing across the cobbled quayside to the sign, which said "Rita's Boutique."

'Yes, but he does not live here with us in the flat. There are complications in my father's business affairs and he wants me to help him. I have experience in investment banking.' I decided to tell Meila about the possible drug smuggling.

'I've reported to CID that there appears to be drugs coming ashore with the cool boxes into Sea View.

'No that surely can't be true.' Meila raised her hand to her mouth in disbelief. They're coming ashore from Babbacombe beach, but then probably nothing to do with the killings at Elberry cove,

'That's really shocking to hear that and that I was working as receptionist while drugs were being delivered to the hotel. It's incredible to think that there could ever be drug smuggling in a small seaside town.' I continued explaining how this came about.

'Marie showed me a letter,' I said, 'which she found in Alfie's diary.

It never got sent to her. It described how he thought that there might be drugs secreted in the bottom compartment of the cool boxes.

'You have done the right thing telling CID about what you've found out. You have no need to do anything else, Phill-ip. You have told the police about the drugs. They are sure to investigate everything thoroughly. I would rather you did nothing more, because I worry about you Phill-ip after all that has happened.

'Have you told Maria about this?

'Yes, I spoke to her about it on my phone.' Meila stood up. There were tears in her eyes. I got up and walked to the other side of the table. I took her in my arms. We kissed. Afterwards she said

'It will all pass over and we can be together. I will speak with Maria. She will understand, when I speak to her, that Babbacombe is not a good place to be in, just now. For now, I have to leave for Spain with my father on business.'

'That is all very sudden.' I held her by the waist not wanting to let go.

'Not really. He has to adapt to market situations, as they occur. To be in the right place at the right time.

'I've no intention of seeing anymore of the police unless I have to,' I said reassuringly. I was back with Meila and for that moment I felt that I was still very much part of her life.

'I'll keep quiet about the drugs in the cool boxes, to everyone else, if that's what you want.' When she embraced me, I reached up to feel the smoothness of the long black hair that flowed down from her shoulders.

'Thank you, Phill-ip. I will always love you for this.' It was the last time that we kissed.

Chapter 48

WE WERE TOGETHER NO longer than half an hour. It seemed shorter than this. The Rendezvous stayed open late to capture ferry passengers arriving from nearby beaches.

A couple arrived while we stood outside the café. We parted from the embrace.

'Will you message?' I asked. 'I mean from Spain.

'No, it is best that I do not straight away. It is best that you do not either.'

'It's goodbye then.' I felt saddened.

'Believe me Phill-ip it is not what I want, but it is how it has to be—for now.' It was re-assuring. Not a total break. The words, at the time felt comforting, with Meila speaking like this hope still existed.

My phone pinged on my way back to the flat in the car. I didn't take any notice, but once parked in Acacia Avenue I looked at it. There was a message from Maria, but I didn't read it. I made coffee like an automaton once in the flat, unable to relax. The news from Meila hit home. I wanted to be out of the flat. I met Debbie on the stairs of the flat going down. I managed a "hi Debs," but kept walking and out on to the Downs. My mind was still processing what Meila said. She was both Meila and Pamela. There was also the name Tom-kins on her email, but she was addressed as Miss Evans when we went to the Blue Comet. I should have asked Meila about this. I walked across the Downs now in a confused state.

Everyone has secrets. Events in their lives, which in retro-spect they would rather didn't define them. Mistakes, errors of judgement, past decisions made, only later to be regretted. I felt a hammer like blow to my chest, when I stopped to lean against the railings. I fell in love with Meila when I first went into Sea View and saw her talking to a guest from behind reception. I did feel that her love for me was genuine. That she felt the same way about me, but now there were secrets. She appeared genuinely upset, yet also there was so much I needed to know that she hadn't told me at the café. I left the footpath along the downs and climbed the steps to the balcony

The balcony, where I first met Maria. The chairs were gone. The white tops of the waves crashed across the darkening cliffs below. Over the railings it was a near vertical drop through bush and small trees that must struggle to grip the red sandstone.

That symmetry I thought to exist between us now thrown apart. I believed that Meila had good reasons for not telling me about what was happening in her life. At the start she did not appear to be hiding anything from me. Now she was leaving the country.

I looked below at the waves dashing into the rocks. My life, now in turmoil from this meeting at the café with Meila. That she was leaving the country and that we could no longer even stay in contact. This was now my situation. A giddiness that you can experience when looking down from a great height came over me. The railings were not insurmountable. It would be quick and sudden. 'Phil,' Maria's voice penetrated my thoughts. I turned. Maria walked further up the steps on to the balcony.

'What are you doing out here? I've been trying to contact you. I phoned you an hour ago.

'It's Pamela,' I said, but checked myself before continuing. 'She's leaving tomorrow. I won't see her again.'

'Yes, she phoned me. I came over from Cliff Side. I was worried about you Phil. I met a girl at your flat. She said that you were out on the Downs. Are you all, right? – no obviously not! She answered her own question.

'Look Phil, I've been talking with Pamela and I agreed with her that you've done the right thing in reporting what you discovered to the Chief Inspector who was staying at Sea View.

'I don't really want to stay here now.' Maria continued without replying directly.

'Pamela said that she doesn't want to leave and go to Spain, either.'

'Did she really?' This raised me from the depths.

'But it is to do with her family and now she's worried that you may be at risk.'

'At risk from what?'

'After she left, she said she thought about the experiences you have been through. That maybe you could be seen as a threat to some local criminal group. The discovery of the bodies and the drugs going into Sea View we agreed were probably not connected, but that there might be people either on the beach or in the hotel, who benefitted from the drug smuggling – come down from the balcony Phil it's chilly standing up here.'

I followed Maria down the steps and I sat next to her on one of the benches to the side of the balcony. She continued. 'You've put a stop to their lucrative operation. Pamela said that maybe something did happen to Alfie. It is possible, if the gang discovered he knew about the contents of the cool boxes that they felt threatened.

– 'But Maria – he died of natural causes it was said—a heart attack.'

'Heart attacks can be caused from severe shock. I realized what Pamela was had said made sense. Maybe Alfie did die of a heart attack. I agree with Pamela that now you've been to the police it's best to let them do their job and make the necessary investigations. I came to pay my respects to Alfie. Nothing we do can bring him back.

You've just said Phil that you don't want to stay here. You don't have to. How would you like to visit Galway?'

'Who with?'

'Me, of course, who else do you think?' At that time and with the ways things were, it was an offer I felt unable to refuse.

'What'll I do?'

'You can stay with me and my aunt. She's a postmistress. There are spare rooms. She takes in tourists. Pamela says that you paint and there's some lovely scenery.

'Do you mean that Maria?'

'I wouldn't be asking you if I didn't mean it Phil!' It was very generous of Maria. There might be some truth in what Pamela had said to Maria. I was comforted in thinking that this was what Meila probably wanted.

'Come away Phil, don't let yourself be upset about something you can't change. It was a holiday romance with Pamela. Wasn't it?'

'I suppose it was.'

I looked out across the railings towards the sea. It was now black, but there was a halo around the moon.

The End

Other Books by Sam Grant

Please check out these other publications by Sam Grant.
Follow blogs, poems and stories at
Samgrantpublications.wordpress.com
Sam Grant, Author – Facebook.

Atlantic Hijack (978-1-78222-291-0)

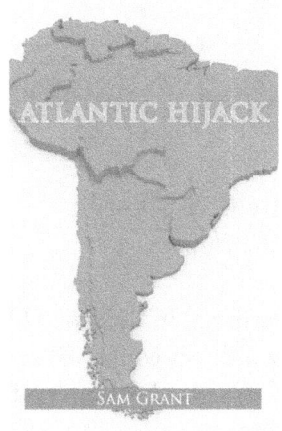

Action, mystery
Sea adventure in the South Atlantic
A secure orderly passage aboard a cargo liner is Ripped apart by a brutal terrorist attack. Author Sam Grant brings his professional seafaring experience to Bear in this thriller that sounds all too familiar from Our evening news bulletins. Apprentice Mike Peters is finding his feet amongst a cast of nautical characters as the Albany Princess voyages to Montevideo. But the ship's personnel are not all that they make themselves out to be as revealed during a rapidly unravelling hijack in the South Atlantic.

River Escape (978-1-68222-574-4)
Sequel to *Atlantic Hijack.*
Action, mystery,
Venezuela: An oil terminal in the River Orinoco, Venezuela. Following on from a military coup. Mike's pressured efforts to prepare the tanker for the load of boiler oil – compromised by a refinery postponement.
An influential young woman, boards who starts calling, the shots? Hidden identity of a rescued yachtsman and two female companions further compromises the ship's safety ...

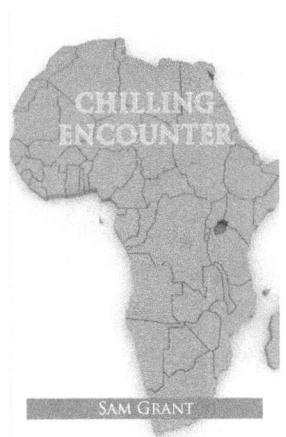

Chilling Encounter (978-1-78222-945-2)
Sequel to *Atlantic Hijack*.
Action, mystery,
Destination: Lagos, Nigeria. Refrigerated liner Albany Contessa on voyage - a part cargo of gold ingots, hidden within machinery cases, aboard. Mike is the newly appointed staff Captain.
A Coaster rescue endangers lives aboard. Leads into further attack with shooting, and need for Foreign Office intervention to avoid international conflict.

Persuasion's Price (978-1-78222-687-1)
Mystery thriller
A quiet market town in England is shattered by an explosive mix of gang rivalry and shady deals. A family is torn apart and, with the involvement of the secret services, events take an unexpected and sinister turn.

Persuasion's Price
The Play (978-1-78222-870-7)
Play, in ten acts. Includes full script and stage instructions ready for rehearsal. Drama group requires curtained stage.
Back stage management has six-scene preparation.
Cast of thirty-two, with possible, actor duplication for smaller parts.
Ninety minutes run time, plus interval.
Brief Summary:
Believed to be hidden in quiet market town away from prying eyes. Anton, son of a Russian family is confronted by secret service. Discovery of illegal smuggling, leads to deal being struck.
Meanwhile, an overseas ransom is offered for kidnap of farmer's daughter.

Galactic Mission (978-1 78222-512-6)
Science fiction
It is 2110. In an advanced technological world of holograms transmitted by mobile phones; food made by a Maxi Maker, drone trays, clones and automata concierges, QUADRANT is the world government. But the world is not at ease and rela-

tionships are put under strain. James Walters is a sales manager for an international conglomerate, based in the UK. One day he encounters Adriana – "The Empress Adriana" – from the Galactic Command Force ...oh, and ruler of planet Earth and all Planets Force, with help from some Inspiring sources thwart planetary conflict.

Galactic Mission Part Two (978-1-78222-773-1
Science fiction, sequel to Galactic Mission
In this classic sci-fi adventure, the main characters from Galactic Mission, including the Empress Adriana, are working to divert comets away from Earth by firing a missile from Mars.

Adriana, has decided to stay in human form, but seeks a closer relation-ship with James, who prefers Lara. He backs away. Adriana is restricted in power. Although Captain Dryson and Alfredo – two android machines – carry out her instructions. After the comets are directed away from earth, Galactic Force returns with Antar-XP200, and two new androids, to replace Adriana, on Mars.

Adriana regains full power and a chosen group leaves for earth by spaceship with the intention of gaining control over Quadrant, who are returning, now that earth has been saved.

Poetry and short story publications by Sam Grant

Poems with themed notes (978-1-78222-464-8)
Love Starved by Electronics is a sonnet selected for a 'Sonnets for Shakespeare' anthology.
In *Riding Through Time* ghostly horsemen appear to ride down the ages.
Captured into their Realm – a meeting with an alien depicted in verse.
Eye of the Storm; The Time Makers Kingdom; Thankful Thoughts and *Spirit of Spring.* These are a few of the poems in this varied anthology.
Notes have been prepared and included by Sam Grant to give background information and set the poems in context.

Mists of Time (978-1-78222-708-3)
From epic poem to scary short story, *Mists of Time* entertains and enlightens. In the title poem, author Sam Grant takes us on a journey. Perhaps his journey, down a leafy lane to a farm

in summer, off to sea and beyond.

Secret Cave is a short story informed by a love of sail boat sailing, a reflection from the author's young life, before the author embarked on a career in the Merchant Service.

Part One – Poems both in traditional and modern form. Dramatic, but also light-hearted topics explored.

Part Two – Short stories.

Individual cameo chapters.

Sam Grant, Author

URL *amazon.com/author/grantsam*

samgrantpublications.wordpress.com

Books are available from good bookshops. Please give ISBN.

Ebook versions on Amazon Kindle store worldwide.